Contents

PAGE 14

PAGE 41

PAGE 88

PAGE 80

FICTION

My Weekly Annual 2011

PAGE 110

PAGE 134

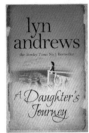
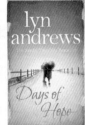
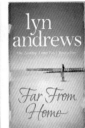
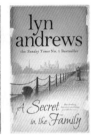

The Best Christmas Ever!

The war was over – but how could they celebrate with too few rations, little money – and no dad…?

By top novelist Lyn Andrews

"Do you think that now the war is over, Mam, this Christmas I can ask Santa for a casie?" Young Billy Dobson gazed up at his mother, his dark eyes filled with hope.

He'd wanted a real football for as long as he could remember. A big leather one all nicely stitched just like the ones that were used by Liverpool and Everton footballers.

The only ball he and his mates had was made up of a bundle of old rags. If he had a "casie", he'd be the envy of every lad in the neighbourhood, but every time he'd asked, his Mam had explained that, because of the war and all the shortages, it just wasn't possible. But this year surely things would be different?

Nora looked at him and her heart sank. How could she refuse him yet again? He didn't have much – they didn't have much – but Billy hardly ever complained. How could she tell him that she just didn't have the money? A case ball, referred to by all the lads as a "casie", would cost far more than she could afford. And, despite the fact that the war, that had lasted for six long, terrifying years, was finally over, food and nearly every other commodity was still in short supply and what was available was rationed.

lyn andrews

The Best Christmas Ever!

"Maybe it would be better if you left it until next year, Billy. Things are bound to be almost back to normal by then," she advised, trying to sound bright and cheerful.

"Ah, Mam! That's ages and ages to wait!" Billy cried, unable to hide his disappointment.

Nora sighed. "Well, we'll see."

"Can I at least write to him and just ask?" he begged. "There's no harm in asking, is there?"

She hadn't the heart to refuse, he looked so earnest. "I don't suppose there is. Now, off you go and play with your mates. I've to go down to the corner shop to see what I can get for our tea." She picked up her

don't know what we're going to do for Christmas, Betty. You still can't get any kind of luxuries, even if I had the money for them. But I was hoping to try and put on some kind of a decent spread for Billy and me."

"Still no sign of your Harry getting home, then?" Betty asked. Nora shook her head. Harry had been taken prisoner four and a half years ago. She been informed by the War Office that he was being held in a camp somewhere in Germany. After VE Day, back in May, she'd hoped he would soon have been repatriated – she wanted him home and so did Billy. After all, thousands of men had

"I don't know what we're going to do for Christmas, Betty." Nora sighed

purse and the ration book from the top of the dresser, pulled on her old coat and tied her scarf under her chin. Billy went off to join the other lads who were playing around the street lamp in the winter dusk.

Marsden's wasn't a big shop and thankfully it wasn't crowded and Betty Marsden soon put the few items Nora had asked for on the counter and had torn the necessary coupons from the ration book. Nora sighed as she handed over the money for her purchases. "I

been de-mobbed now.

She'd had a couple of letters from him since then, in which he'd explained that things in Germany and France were still chaotic, but that he was well and was looking forward to seeing both her and Billy again and that he'd missed them terribly.

"I'd really hoped he would be back home with us this year, Betty, but still I should be thankful that he is coming back; so many won't be."

Betty nodded. It had been so hard on all the wives and mothers

They used a bundle of rags for a ball

and for many the grief at the loss of loved ones would last a lifetime.

Nora continued, "And just before I came out, our Billy asked could he have a real casie for Christmas. He's had his heart set on one for years and I just couldn't say no again, but he's going to be so disappointed on Christmas morning, Betty. It's going to be hard enough to find the money for a few cheap toys, never mind a proper football. Poor little lad, it's not going to be much of a Christmas for him again."

Betty nodded looking thoughtful. "I've got an idea. You're handy with a needle, Nora, and before the war your Harry worked in the tannery. Why don't you go down there and see that foreman Jim Blake? You always said that Harry got on well with him. Ask him can he get you a few pieces of leather – off-cuts or something like that."

Nora brightened up. "I could cut them into shape and sew them together with a sailmaker's needle."

"And you could stuff it with rags or straw," Betty added enthusiastically as Nora put her groceries into her shopping bag.

"I'll go and see him this evening. Thanks, Betty."

After they'd eaten and Nora had cleared away, she told Billy she was just popping out to one of the neighbours and he could amuse himself by writing his letter to Santa Claus as she wouldn't be long.

She hurried through the cold, dark streets to the tannery, for they worked late into the night. The place stank but she tried to ignore it.

"Nora Dobson. What brings you down here at this time? Any news of Harry?" the middle-aged foreman asked.

"Only that he's well and hoping to be home soon. It's our Billy." She bit her lip.

"Missing his dad?"

Nora nodded. "And he's asking Santa for a real casie and I just can't afford one, so I was wondering if… well… if I could buy a few pieces of leather? Off-cuts or bits that aren't much good and I'll try to make him a football."

He nodded slowly. "Come and see me tomorrow evening and I'll see what I can do – and don't you be worrying about payment. Can't have the lad down in the dumps at Christmas, now, can we?"

Nora smiled and impulsively kissed him on the cheek. "Oh, thank you. I've got to try and make it a bit special for him, haven't I?"

When she arrived home Billy was folding up his letter.

"I've written to Santa, Mam. I've told him that I will be really, really grateful if I can have one, but that if he can't manage it this year maybe he'll put my name at the top of his list for next year."

She ruffled his hair affectionately. "That's the thing to do all right, Billy, but I think he just might be able to manage it this year."

His face lit up. "Really, Mam? Do you?"

Nora nodded. "Right then, let's send this letter off."

Delightedly Billy pushed the letter up the chimney and Nora helped it on its way with the poker.

Before he switched off his bedside light, Billy looked, as he always did, at the photo of his father in his RAF uniform that sat in its frame on the little chest beside his bed.

It had been taken before he'd

gone off to fight and he looked proud and was smiling. That was how Billy always tried to remember him, but it seemed so long ago now that he could barely remember what his father's voice sounded like, and he was sure that without the photo he'd have trouble remembering what he even looked like.

Every night he said his prayers, asking that God would keep his Dad safe and well and that he'd be home again soon.

"I think this year I'm really going to get that football, Dad," he

For three nights she worked while Billy slept

confided to the photo before switching off the light.

The following evening, Jim Blake handed Nora a small parcel and she thanked him again and returned home. For the next three nights when Billy was asleep she worked hard. She shaped the

She had obtained a very small piece of lamb that she would cook with carrots and potatoes for lunch tomorrow. There would be no traditional plum pudding or mince pies, she thought, but she hoped next year things would be different.

Billy woke early; he'd been so excited he'd hardly slept. It was

She sewed the strips neatly together, even though it made her fingers bleed

odd pieces of leather into strips and sewed them neatly together with strong twine threaded through a curved sailmaker's needle.

When she had nearly finished, she stuffed the ball tightly with straw and sewed up the remaining gap in the seam. She smiled and nodded to herself as she studied her handiwork. She'd made a really good job of it and she didn't even mind the fact that her fingers were sore and bleeding. He'd be delighted with it.

On Christmas Eve she managed to get a couple of small, cheap toys and she had an apple, a shiny new penny and – miraculously – an orange for Billy, too. She put up the little tree and decorated it and hung paper chains across the kitchen ceiling. The red and gold glittery sign (now a bit battered) that read *Happy Christmas* was perched over the mirror that hung above the range.

still dark and he wondered what time it was. Was it too early? Had Santa been? The room was cold but he threw back the bedclothes and switched on the light, scrambling to the bottom of the bed where he'd hung the small pillowcase which Mam had said would serve better than a stocking. Eagerly, with mounting excitement, he felt around inside it.

There were two small round shapes which proved to be an apple and an orange, something he hadn't tasted for a long time. Then there were two square objects which turned out to be a brightly painted pencil box and a pack of three small toy soldiers. His fingers closed over a coin; a bright, shiny new penny and then… nothing!

He sat on the bed looking at the small collection. His heart felt like a lump of lead and tears of bitter disappointment stung his eyes. There was no football. Santa hadn't left him one.

"Is this what you're searching for, Billy?"

He looked up, puzzled and surprised at hearing a man's voice. He hadn't heard a man's voice in the house for years and years.

Then he saw the football. Santa hadn't forgotten! It was a real casie, proper leather and all neatly sewn – and his dad was holding it out to him. His dad!

> ## "Is this what you're searching for, Billy?" He was surprised by a man's voice

He blinked through his tears, wondering if he was dreaming, then he launched himself toward his father.

"Dad! Dad! You've come home!"

Harry Dobson hugged his son tightly to him. All the years of imprisonment, humiliation, hardship and deprivation were behind him. There had been times when he'd despaired of ever seeing his home and his beloved wife and son again but all that was over now.

He dashed away the tears that trickled down his still gaunt cheeks as Nora put her arms around them both, her face glowing with pure joy.

"Sorry to make you wait for your

Who was holding his football?

casie, son, but your mam thought it would be a much better surprise if I gave it to you."

Billy beamed with happiness, clutching the football tightly to him with one arm while he hung onto his father just as tightly with the other one.

"This is going to be the best Christmas ever, Dad!"

Harry kissed them both. "It most certainly is, Billy."

Lyn Andrews

Who is your inspiration?
My inspiration is Catherine Cookson. She was so prolific and wrote until her death a few years ago. Her love of her native Tyneside always came through, as I hope mine does for my native city of Liverpool which has provided me a wonderful background for my novels.

What makes you cry?
I always cry watching the Remembrance Sunday parade at the Cenotaph and when I see yet another coffin coming through Wooton Bassett it makes me cry. War is such a terrible waste of young lives.

Where are you most at home?
I am equally at home here in Ireland where I do all my writing or in Southport when I am closer to my family.

When are you happiest?
I'm happiest when I have all four of my grandchildren around me

Author of 26 bestsellers

lyn andrews
A Daughter's Journey

lyn andrews
A Secret in the Family

and on our annual family holiday. All twelve of us go away together for a week each year, usually to somewhere hot, and it's lovely to have my daughter and her family and my two sons and their families around us for a week. As my daughter lives in the south of England, it's also great for her to spend time with her brothers.

> **"I hope my love for my native city of Liverpool comes through in my novels"**

Christmas And Coleen

Our favourite Loose Woman tells us what makes Christmas such a special time of year for her…

What did you love about Christmas as a child?
Waiting for Santa! I thought he would never come. Also seeing all the presents under the tree. It was and is my favourite time of year!

Please tell us your most special Christmas memory as a mum.
My favourite Christmas memory as a mum is always Christmas Eve, lighting the fire then sitting down in our pyjamas and watching a Christmas film.

Then trying to get kids to sleep when they're so excited they're about to burst. First thing in the morning running round shouting, "He's been! He's been!"

Tell us one thing you do to make your family's Christmas special.
I always have a Christmas CD playing in the morning while they open their presents – and Santa always leaves a letter to them in the chimney!

What drives you nuts at Christmas?
People telling me what to do. What time dinner should be on the table, that you should dress up for it, and sometimes having to be with people that you don't see all year but you have to because it's Christmas!

Do you have a secret way to ensure a relaxing Christmas?
My tip for relaxing is to remember to enjoy it because Christmas is only one day. You're with people you love and who love you; if you burn the turkey, so what! It's your day too, remember that!

● *Envy* By Coleen Nolan published by Pan (£7.99)

Christmas is a family time for Coleen

I love Christmas, thanks to my mum and dad. They always made it magical

On The Loose

Those other Loose Women let us in on their little family traditions for a perfect day…

Lynda Bellingham

I just love Christmas decorations. Every year I try to be good, and use the same ones again, but every year I get led astray by some new light or table decoration.

Jane McDonald

We've got a piano in the lounge, and we all sit down and have a singsong. It's very traditional.

Lisa Maxwell

I want to make sure all my friends and family get that Christmas feeling – I have a tree in every room in the house!

Lesley Garrett

Our most important tradition is wearing the family pyjamas, which are covered in reindeer.

From a sing-song around the piano to a tree in every room, family traditions are important

Teatime Treats

FUN, TASTY BAKES

Lemon Drizzle Cup Cakes

Ingredients

- 125g (4oz) butter, softened
- 200g (7oz) caster sugar
- Finely grated zest of two lemons
- 2 large eggs, beaten
- 200g (7oz) self-raising flour
- ½ tsp baking powder
- 100ml (4fl oz) milk

For the lemon drizzle:

- Juice of 2 lemons
- 100g (4oz) granulated sugar
- Crystallised or edible flowers, to decorate

Preparation time: 35mins
Cooking time: 7-10mins
Makes: 12-16

FAMILY FAVOURITE

● Preheat the oven to 180˚C, Fan Oven 160˚C, Gas Mark 4. Set 12 paper cases in a 12 hole bun or muffin tin.

● Cream the **butter** and **sugar** with the **lemon zest** until pale and fluffy. Beat in the **eggs**, splash by splash. If the mixture looks curdled, beat in a tablespoon of the **flour**. Sift the flour and **baking powder**, then fold into the mix alternately with the **milk**.

● Spoon the mixture into the paper cases – about ¾ full – and bake for 25mins. Tip out on to a wire rack. Prick all over. Quickly mix the **lemon juice** and **sugar** together, swirling so the sugar doesn't completely dissolve.

● Spoon over each warm cake – it will seep into the holes, leaving a delicate sugar crust on the surface. Decorate with **flowers** and eat the same day.

RECIPE AND STYLING: MAXINE CLARK
PHOTOGRAPHY: UPFRONT PHOTOGRAPHY

Santa And The Stork

Your heart will go out to this bewildered little mite – and the spinster, with whom she's hastily left…

By Margaret Waddingham

That date I'll never forget. My parents left me on Christmas Eve, 1951. I was four at the time and it had been snowing all day.

They left me – or, to be more precise, my father left me – next door with Miss Robinson. Kissing me, he told me to be a good girl, and said that they'd be back soon.

It had all happened quite near tea time, when my mother, who was making mince pies with me helping, went all peculiar; sort of doubled up with a moan and a strange look on her face.

"Sally, phone Daddy quickly," she gasped, sitting down in a heap.

Someone else answered and I said, "I want my daddy."

A voice said, "Is that you, Sal?"

"I want my daddy. Mummy wants him quickly."

When Daddy answered, I told him how Mummy had gone all peculiar and that she needed him to come home. Within minutes, he was bursting through the back door, still in his overalls and cap decorated with snowflakes, and looking all puffed out.

Then the doctor arrived, then an ambulance and, before I knew what was happening, they had left me with Miss Robinson – who was wearing two cardigans, one blue and one green.

She was small and round – round figure, round spectacles, round eyes and a round mouth that went into a round "O" whenever you told her anything to surprise her. She was nice, but I wasn't sure that I liked her enough to be left.

I stood silent and shivering in her chilly hall, a small, hastily packed suitcase at my feet and Impy Bruin Esq clutched to my

Would Santa find me next door?

chest. She smiled at me through her round spectacles and said, "Such a nice surprise, Sally. I was going to be all alone for Christmas, but it looks as though I shall have company after all."

Then it hit me properly. My parents had left me, the day before Father Christmas was due to come with my presents. I don't know what upset me the most – the fact that Father Christmas might not now know where to find me, or that I didn't know why my parents had left me. I burst into tears.

She looked at me in alarm, then put her arm round my shoulders and said, "Oh, my lamb, they'll be back as soon as they can. Come into the sitting-room and I'll go to get some cocoa."

I hated cocoa, but I was too upset to tell her. She pushed me gently into the sitting-room and on to a chair next to the fire. It flickered unhappily, so she stirred it around with a poker and little flames and sparks shot up the chimney. She smiled again, sang, "Cocoa!" and disappeared.

Wiping my nose on the back of my hand, I stared round the room, in which everything seemed to be in shades of blue and brown. A large clock ticked in a steadying, dull sort of way in a corner, a jug of holly was set in the middle of a table in the window and three Christmas cards stood on the otherwise bare mantelpiece.

I thought it all looked very dull compared with my house, which had things in lots of colours, cards crammed along the tops of all surfaces, paper chains laboriously made by me and Mummy hanging across the rooms and little sprigs of holly, picked by Daddy and me, tucked behind each picture.

I felt tears on my cheeks again, and I wiped them away on Impy

I didn't know what was going on

Bruin Esq's soft comforting ears.

Miss Robinson brought in the cocoa and we sat on each side of the fire with it.

She said, "I know it's strange, Mummy and Daddy having to go off so unexpectedly – and on one of the best days of the year – but when they come home, I wouldn't be surprised if they don't have a beautiful present for you."

"Will it be a doll's pram?" I asked hopefully. That's what I had asked for in my letter to Santa.

"It may be even better than that. But in the meantime, we shall have some fun. Tomorrow, if it stops snowing, we'll go for a walk and build a snowman, and we'll sit by the fire and play Ludo and look at some books, and then of course, there's Christmas lunch.

"I've got a chicken to roast and

some sprouts and potatoes – do you like sprouts?" she added quite anxiously I thought.

I shook my head.

"Carrots, then," she said. "You like carrots, I'm sure."

I shook my head again. I was determined not to like anything.

I drank a bit of the cocoa and then gave up. Miss Robinson said, "Shall we go up and see if we can settle you in your room?"

She went ahead up the stairs with my case and I trailed after her, holding Impy Bruin Esq by the paw so that he bumped along beside me. We went into a very cold bedroom.

"Brrr," she said, "it's chilly in here." She lit a little gas fire that fitted neatly in a corner. It was a small room with a brown wardrobe, a brown dressing table, a chair, and a bed covered with a bright orange counterpane. Over the head of the bed was a picture

drawers. Don't worry about the wardrobe. I'll hang things up for you." She effortlessly folded up the counterpane and took it into the bathroom, returning with an armful of sheets, blankets and a pink and blue eiderdown. I was so relieved to see that the orange counterpane had disappeared.

There weren't many things in my case – knickers, vests and socks, a clean liberty bodice and another jumper and skirt, pyjamas and dressing gown. My most favourite dress wasn't there – the deep pink one with smocking that I was going to wear on Christmas Day with a new cardigan that Mummy had knitted for me. I stifled another sob.

Miss Robinson smoothed sheets, tucked in blankets and pushed a pillow into a pillow case.

"Babies do funny things, don't they?" she asked conversationally. "Like making an appearance when they're not really expected."

"I like sherbet fountains, too – but not with roast chicken and roast potatoes"

of a cow, knee-deep in a stream. It looked rather surprised, I thought, as though it didn't know quite how it had got there.

Miss Robinson swished red curtains across the windows and said, "I'll make up the bed while you put your things away in the

I didn't know what she was talking about so I watched her pushing the pillow until she stopped and looked hard at me.

"You did know your mummy's having a baby, didn't you, Sally?"

"She said she might, one day," I said, and we both fell silent.

Miss Robinson's face had gone all pink and an awful thought had come into my mind.

You see, I remember Mummy asking if I would like a baby brother or sister, but Auntie Bessie had been to see us a few days before and I had overheard them talking. What I'd heard made me none too sure that I wanted either, for quite a long time, so I had said,

decided to arrive in such a hurry that your Mummy had to go to hospital for him."

I stared in astonishment, then said, "Is she ill?"

"No, it's just that they both wanted a bit of help and, what with the snow and everything, your mummy and daddy thought it would be best if you stayed with me because your grandparents

"This baby's in a hurry, you see; your mummy had to go to hospital for him"

"Not yet, thank you very much."

She had laughed a bit and said, "I didn't mean immediately, you silly billy. But perhaps one day, quite soon?"

"All right," I'd agreed, "one day."

It hadn't been mentioned much after that. Mummy kept knitting things that were much too small for me. She said they were for the baby. She put them in a spare drawer in my room and then one evening, when Daddy came home with a wooden crib, that was put in my room, too. They said this was for the baby, but that my doll could sleep in it for the time being.

I asked Miss Robinson when Mummy and Daddy would come back for me, and she said the most surprising thing.

"That all depends on when the baby comes along. This one has

couldn't get here in time."

I clutched Impy Bruin Esq, trying to take everything in. Miss Robinson gave the eiderdown a final tweak and said brightly, "We'll leave the fire on until you're in bed, so that the room will be all cosy for you. We'll go down and get some supper now, and then you can have a nice warm bath and before you know it – Christmas morning will be here!"

We had almost finished eating our scrambled eggs and toast, when we heard the sound of singing outside.

"Oh, listen," Miss Robinson said. "Isn't that nice? Carol singers."

The singers finished *Away In A Manger*, then knocked at the door. Miss Robinson opened it and five children stood there, three girls muffled up in pixie hoods and mittens and two small boys in warm woolly balaclava helmets.

They began again. "*We wish you a merry Christmas*," they piped, "*we wish you a merry Christmas…*" They stood there hopefully, letting in cold air and little swirls of snow.

"Come in, come in," beamed Miss Robinson. "I've got some mince pies just out of the oven."

They trooped after her into the kitchen, and she got a plateful from the larder and passed it round. "Isn't this really nice, Sally?" she beamed with enjoyment.

I nodded mutely but refused a mince pie. I wondered if they'd knocked on our door.

"There's no one in next door," I said, and then said it again in case they hadn't heard.

Miss Robinson seemed to be enjoying herself. She stood amidst the circle of children and they sang *Away In A Manger* all over again,

Would Santa bring me anything here?

and when she asked them what they were hoping to receive for Christmas, they gave her their lists – Biggles books, beads, pink slippers, a cricket bat, a grown-up shoulder bag.

When they had gone, clutching pennies she had found for them, she said, "Now, Sally, we must remember to hang up your stocking for Father Christmas."

I stared at her again. What was the point? He wasn't going to bring me anything, was he? Surely she realised that he wouldn't know where I was.

I snuffled into Impy Bruin Esq's dark-brown fur and she took me gently by the hand and led me upstairs to the bathroom.

Miss Robinson pulled a switch for a wall heater to do its work and while I undressed, a noisy gas geyser gushed hot water on top of some crystals that made the water green and smell funny.

I splashed around disconsolately for a few minutes, refusing offers of help, then she rubbed me down briskly and helped me to put on my pyjamas, warm from the airing cupboard. Then we pinned one of my socks on the wall by the bed.

I looked at it without hope. I could only remember one other Christmas – the preceding one – and then my sock had been filled with exciting things the next morning. This time, I knew it would be as empty in the morning as it was when we hung it up.

"You must be tired out, my lamb," said Miss Robinson. The little bedroom felt quite snug now and the bed was warmed by a stone hot water bottle.

"Snuggle down," she said. "Would you like me to read you a bedtime story?"

I wasn't sure. I sometimes liked Mummy reading stories in her soft, soothing voice, but most of all, I liked Daddy reading them because he could do funny voices that always made me giggle.

She produced a red book. "I've got the *Just So Stories*. Would you like one of those?"

I nodded, yawned and cuddled Impy Bruin Esq. I was too tired to fight any more.

She opened the book, but before she started reading, she looked at me and stroked my cheek gently. "Poor lamb," she said, "you mustn't worry. They'll be home soon."

I fell asleep half way through *How The Elephant Got Its Trunk* and somehow, although I've since read all the other stories in that book, I have never managed to finish that one without a lump in my throat.

Something was crackling when I moved my feet. I sat up and in the gloom, found the light switch and stared in surprise. Father Christmas had found me after all!

He hadn't forgotten me!

Both, not one, of my socks were on the bed, bulging with strange-looking packages. I began opening them, but almost before I'd begun, Miss Robinson came in dressed in a long green dressing gown, with her head full of hair pins and uncomfortable-looking iron things.

"Happy Christmas, my lamb," she said, kissing the top of my head. "Happy Christmas." She wrapped my dressing gown round my shoulders.

"How did Father Christmas know I was here?" I demanded, wrestling with paper and string to reveal a pale-coloured little purse with a brown camel on it and a threepenny bit inside.

"Oh, I managed to catch him," she explained, "and tell him where you were."

In the socks were all manner of

excitements. A little soap dish with flowers painted on the top; a pencil with a rubber in the end; a beautiful clip for my hair, shaped like a butterfly; a tiny silver thimble; a hanky with embroidered flowers; a shiny notebook; some coloured beads; some bright red hair ribbon, enough for both my bunches; a soap in the shape of a swan, and two tangerines – one in the toe of each sock.

"He's brought me some very nice things," I said. "Just what I wanted." It didn't occur to me until I was quite a lot older that most of these presents were quite adult things.

"He's clever like that, you know. Now then, what would you like for your breakfast? Porridge, perhaps, or a boiled egg and soldiers?"

I felt suddenly hungry. "Could I please have some golden syrup on a little porridge?"

"Of course you can." She beamed. "Can you get yourself dressed, or would you like some help?"

Esq, "Miss Robinson is very nice and everything, but I don't really want to have to stay here forever and ever."

He looked at me with his shiny brown eyes and agreed. I felt the little hard disk that used to be his growl. "Does it hurt, now it won't growl any more?" I whispered, but he didn't want to answer and I thought how brave he was – and that if he was brave, then so should I be about being left by my mummy and daddy.

I heard the telephone ring in the hall and then Miss Robinson's voice answering it.

She had dressed in a bright red dress and a green cardigan, thick stockings, and slippers that slapped on the linoleum every time she walked. Her hair was out of its metal things and was arranged in a lot of tight little curls all round her forehead.

"I've got something exciting to

"Oh, yes – I managed to catch Father Christmas, and tell him where you are"

"I can do most of it except my hair. I like it in bunches, but they always escape when I try to do it."

"That's all right, my lamb. We'll do it after breakfast. Don't forget to wash, now, will you?"

As I dressed, I said to Impy Bruin

tell you!" she exclaimed, as she put the bowl of porridge and the green and gold tin of syrup before me. "Your special present has arrived – a baby brother."

I think my mouth fell open.

"Don't you think that is a lovely

present for you on Christmas Day?"

"I thought it wasn't going to come until I wanted it to," I said at last.

Her mouth did its little "O". "Why did you think that?"

I made the syrup leave little golden trails in my porridge. I could hardly bear to ask the question that had been troubling me.

"Will I be living here all the time now? Because of this new baby brother I've been given?"

Her mouth formed an even bigger "O" now.

"Goodness me, no," she said. "They'll be wanting you back home with them just as soon as possible. What made you think that you would have to stay here for longer than a day or so?"

at all hungry any more.

"Do you know," she said suddenly, "I think you might have mistaken what your Auntie Bessie was trying to say.

"I think she was just saying that since she had to stay in bed for a while, it was better for young Geoffrey if he went away to stay with some relations until she was well enough to look after both him and the new baby properly. I don't think she meant that he was going away forever. I think he's probably back home again now."

"You do?" I said doubtfully.

"I do," she said in a very positive sort of way.

"But all the baby's things are in my room, so I thought that meant

"May I see your nice present?" I asked. She smiled. "Look in the mirror. It's you"

"Because my Auntie Bessie said she wouldn't have been able to manage her Geoffrey and a new baby so Geoffrey had to go away for a while."

"And how long did Geoffrey have to stay away for?"

"I don't know." I was getting very miserable and upset now.

"But when did your auntie have this lovely little new baby?"

"I don't know," I repeated.

Miss Robinson was quiet for a few moments while I looked at my porridge. All of a sudden, I wasn't

What a lucky girl!

it would be his room and I'd be going away."

She laughed with more than a little relief now. "That's because your daddy's painting the little room for him. You knew he was painting it, didn't you?"

Yes, I did know that, I remembered. He had painted it a lovely shade of yellow, and I'd noticed he'd just about finished it before all of this "excitement" had begun the day before.

I said hesitantly, "So, won't I be living with you all the time?"

Miss Robinson smiled her gentle smile again behind her big round and friendly spectacles.

"There's nothing I'd like better, but I think your mummy and daddy will want you back as soon as possible. I've just sort of borrowed you, until they can get back through the snow. And it's stopped, now – so that might be tomorrow or the day after."

"Will he be all wrinkly and cry a lot, my new brother?" I asked.

"They're mostly wrinkly when they're new, and they cry because they can't talk like me and you, but they soon learn."

Suddenly, I wanted more than anything to meet this baby brother who had come in time to be my special Christmas present.

"I'd like to see him, I think," I said and began to eat my porridge.

She nodded. "Of course you would. In the meantime, you're going to stay with me for a bit longer, just until they get home. Will you mind that terribly?"

I thought about this for quite a long time. I thought about Miss Robinson who had let Father Christmas know where I was, and I thought about the carol singers she had been so pleased to see. And I thought about her, living alone in her house with only three Christmas cards, and I said, "Miss Robinson, have you got a nice present? What did Father Christmas bring you?"

She sucked in her cheeks, making "O"s of her mouth and her eyes all at once. "He doesn't usually send grown-ups presents, but this year he did."

"May I see?"

"Look in the mirror." She smiled. "It's you."

I was only four. There was so much I didn't understand. Yet even then, I must have felt some sense of Miss Robinson and her lonely life, for I said, "Miss Robinson, Impy Bruin Esq thinks he might like to try carrots and Christmas pudding after all."

FROM THE AUTHOR

"The Impy Bruin Esq in this story is my bear. He hasn't got much fur now and his expression is rather sad, but I still love him."

Growing P

The strangest little coincidences can be the most memorable things on the path to adulthood…

By Brenda Crickmar

oby thought he'd never felt so miserable in all his eleven-and-three-quarter years. He knew he wasn't the only kid whose parents got divorced. He knew deep down that Mum and Dad both still loved him, even if they didn't love each other any more. It just felt as though between them they'd managed to ruin his life.

It had felt bad enough that they'd called him Toby – called him Toby and given him ginger hair on top! What sort of a name was Toby? It was a dog's name – that was what. And ginger hair? It was all very well Mum calling it auburn and saying it would go darker with time. When was that going to be, was what he'd like to know? Exactly when? Every morning he'd look for signs in the mirror but it hadn't happened yet.

And now on top of everything else, this divorce thing.

Of course, he'd known it was coming, in a way. It had started with the rows, then the not speaking and then a period of relative calm, which had lulled Toby into a false sense of security. But then – pow! The packing up of their things – Mum's and his. The dismantling of his computer, the rolling up of his football posters, and then: the move.

"I don't see why we have to go," grumbled Toby. "Why doesn't *he* go? There's only the one of him."

"Because I've got Nan's bungalow. She left it to me and it's ideal. Our old house will be sold anyway and with my share we can make the bungalow really nice for us."

Bungalow! What eleven-year-old would be

"I'll help you with the garden, Mum"

ains

seen dead in a bungalow? And what improvements? A skate boarding ramp or a BMX park?

No, he didn't think so. More likely a conservatory, complete with a cute cross-eyed concrete rabbit sitting quietly on the step.

"It's easy maintenance," went on Mum bravely. "It needs a bit of TLC, but you'll see, it'll be great. You'll only have one bus stop to school, or back to Dad's and it's just a short walk round the corner to the supermarket."

Toby's mum was smiling. Smiling! As though having a mum who worked in a supermarket was anything to smile about. As though only one bus stop to school was any big deal. Toby felt almost inconsolable now.

The weekend of the move was sunny but with a hint of the autumn that was just around the corner. Toby and his mum worked hard for two days moving furniture every which way in an effort to make it fit the smaller rooms. "Well, it's cosy," Mum said at the end of it all.

Thinking of his light and airy room in their old house, that overlooked the tree tops of the park where he played football, Toby grunted.

"It's not that bad," Mum said with a fixed smile. "Buck up, Toby, I'm relying on you."

Toby didn't like talking about feelings, so he got up and made her a cup of coffee instead, and when she drew designs on the back of an envelope for the makeover of the garden, he tried hard to look really

Toby bit back the retort that no one else would care either. "Whatever," he said then, seeing his mum's lips compress, "I'll help you, if you like."

Repairing the lawn was hard work. They dug and raked, removed stones, bought topsoil and spread it, raked it again and only then did Mum pronounce it ready for turfing.

A few days later, after a particularly bad physics lesson followed by a small tussle with a particularly obnoxious bully in the year above, Toby arrived

"If we plant bulbs now, it'll look great by spring"

The weekend was sunny and Toby and his mum worked hard on the move

interested and enthusiastic.

"The front lawn's a mess," she admitted. "Nan's old dog dug up most of it and when he was put down, the weeds took over. I think the best bet is to have it re-turfed. If we do it in the autumn it'll look great by spring. We could put some crocuses in it. It will be our secret till spring! No one else will ever know."

home to find a brown paper bag on the kitchen table with a hand-written note lying beside it.

Dear Toby, the note read. *Will be home late tonight, had to change shifts with Shelley. Be an angel and plant these bulbs in the lawn. They need to go in an oval drift. Just push them into the soil a couple of inches and rake the earth*

it upset his sense of order, didn't look quite right, so he spread them out equidistantly in the oval. Then he stood back and surveyed his handiwork. That was much better. What did mothers know? A drift indeed. Not very neat in Toby's opinion. Quickly he covered the bulbs over and feeling rather smug, went inside to wash his hands.

The next morning on his way to school, midway to slamming the front door behind him, he stopped and stared in disbelief at the churned up soil in the front garden. He couldn't have left it in that much of a mess could he? It must have been dogs or cats fighting. *Typical!* thought Toby. Furiously, he scuffed the bulbs back into the ground. So much for his perfect oval. It was all spoiled. With the heavy sigh of an Alan Titchmarsh in the making, he hurried on to school.

back smooth. It won't take long. Need to do it before the turf man comes tomorrow. Thanks, love. Mum xxx

Toby ignored the note, made himself a cheese sandwich with far too much pickle, then got stuck into his computer game. An hour later, he remembered the bulbs, half-heartedly picked up the bag and examined its sorry looking contents. So what exactly was an oval drift meant to look like?

Rolling up the bottoms of his school trousers (he should have changed them by now, but Mum wasn't there to see) bag in hand, he stepped gingerly on to the soil. With his finger he mapped out a rough oval and threw the contents of the bag in the middle. Somehow,

By the time February came, things were looking up for Toby. He'd suddenly grown taller, was scoring goals on the football field, which surprised everyone, most of all him, and his hair really did seem to have darkened a shade. He'd discovered that living in a bungalow wasn't as terrible as it sounded, especially since at the other end of the street a new member of his class had moved in.

The new classmate was a girl. Usually Toby didn't have much truck with girls, but this girl was… well, she was worth thinking about. And Toby thought about her. A lot.

Her name was Lily. She had coffee-coloured skin and round blue eyes with very thick lashes. She also had a way of looking at Toby which made him feel hot and cool, all at the same time. She even told him once that she thought he was pretty cool. Afterwards he'd kicked himself for not saying, "Well, I just think you're pretty." That would have been a really cool thing to say – but no good, of course, two days later.

Mum, on the other hand wasn't doing quite so well. She often said she felt she was getting nowhere. Life was work, work, work, with nothing to look forward to that was out of the ordinary apart from the odd visit to the dentist.

When Toby had said helpfully that that was better than nothing, she'd said that obviously he'd never met the dentist and perhaps it was time he did. Toby kept quiet after that.

Occasionally, because Toby was good at maths and Lily wasn't, Lily would call in on her way home from school and he would help her with her homework. This made Toby feel like a mathematical genius and Lily smile and giggle in a way that was very gratifying.

On one such day, they were sitting in the kitchen eating crisps when Mum came in. Her eyes were shining and she had a broad smile on her face.

"Oh, Toby," she said. "What a wonderful surprise."

"What?" said Toby.

"The crocuses, of course. Didn't you notice them?"

"No," said Toby feeling slightly embarrassed now because, after all

He planted the bulbs in a rough oval

a crocus was only a crocus, nothing to get all watery eyed about.

"Come and look."

Toby wouldn't have bothered only Lily was already on her feet following Mum outside.

Toby stared at the lawn, which was green and lush from the winter, and at first he could see

"Do you?" croaked Toby, blushing madly.

Mum gave Toby a quick hug and disappeared indoors.

"Just one thing," said Toby to Lily before they followed her. "I'd rather you didn't tell anyone at school about the heart thing. Mum's been having a hard time lately, but well, I don't want anyone

Toby and Lily were sitting in the kitchen when Mum came in, her eyes shining

nothing. Then he noticed a few purple tips, then on looking harder a few golden ones.

"That's just so sweet, Toby. Just when I was feeling so low."

"Well, you knew I'd done it," said Toby prosaically. "You asked me to. Wouldn't have done it otherwise, would I?"

"Yes, but to do it like that, darling – it's just so very lovely."

Toby cringed. Then he looked more closely and could see that by some strange fluke the crocuses had arranged themselves in the shape of a heart.

"Um," gulped Toby.

Lily looked at him with shining eyes. "What a lovely thing to do for your mum," she said. "I think that's wonderful!"

to think it's the sort of thing I do all the time. People might think I want to be a flower arranger or something."

Lily leaned towards him and a deliriously happy Toby felt a flutter on his cheek. "I won't tell anyone if you don't want me to. But I think you're just lovely."

"I think so, too," said Toby. "I mean, no, I don't think I'm lovely. No, of course not. It's you. You are. Lovely, I mean. Really lovely."

"Oh, Toby, shut up!" said Lily, laughing.

TRY A POCKET NOVEL

Find a world of romance at all good newsagents and selected Asda/Tesco

My Weekly
Pocket Novel

Heart-stopping Moments

Thrills and Intrigue

Powerful Romance

Handy Size
GREAT READ
Only £1.55

Signs Of Spring

Follow Barbara on an emotional journey from loss to a fresh, new beginning in this emotional story

By Rachel Long

T hat's just what I've been looking for," Barbara declared, reaching out for *Mediterranean Cooking – Flavours of the Sun*.

"Really?" Amy replied, rubbing her pregnant bump. "Why?"

"Because," her mother replied, "I want to cook something exciting, of course." She raised a salt-and-pepper eyebrow. "Why do you think?"

"I don't know – it's just –"

"What?"

"Mediterranean cooking is a little more involved than watching Rick Stein on a canal boat, Mum. And opening a jar of Dolmio with extra garlic doesn't count."

Barbara's lips compressed tightly as she bit her tongue. It was a strange relationship, that of mother and daughter. Their bond was one of the closest there could possibly be, biologically, and their mutual love was unquestionable, but why was it that all children felt they could be so patronising to a parent?

"Your father and I had our moments of culinary adventure, I'll have you know. Your dad even had sea urchins in Italy once." Barbara shot her daughter a "so there" sort of smile and continued to leaf through the glossy pages.

Amy pretended to shudder

It had been five years, but reminders of her dear Tom still caught her unawares

A flutter of wings caught her eye

with disgust and put her arm around her mother's narrow shoulders. "Oh, Mum. I know you miss Daddy – we all do. He was lovely, wasn't he?"

Barbara put the book in her basket and wandered out of the garden centre gift section towards the houseplants. As she turned to admire a particularly glossy fern, an orchid feeder fell at her feet. Bending to pick it up, her glasses slid off and a large packet of Weed and Feed toppled over, spewing its contents over the polished floor. A tear spilled down Barbara's cheek, chilling as it reached her chin and dropped onto her scarf.

"Mum!" Amy exclaimed. "Don't get so upset – accidents happen." Her cheeks flushed as she looked into her mother's sad brown eyes. "Is there something else? Was it something I said?"

"No, darling. It's just me being daft and clumsy." Barbara nodded gratefully at the assistant, armed with dustpan and brush, who waved her away with a reassuring smile. "The little things catch you unawares, sometimes, don't they? Your dad loved his lawn…"

Amy's eyes were suddenly a little shinier. "Come on. Let's have a nice cup of tea."

The tinkle of cutlery on china and the warm gravy-type smell that filled the cosy restaurant was strangely comforting as the two women contemplated the damp, brown twigs and grey flagstones outside.

"I hate this time of year," Barbara grumbled. "It's cold and dark and there's nothing to do except read through seed catalogues all day. I can't wait to get back in the garden again—I feel so much better about everything out there."

"Oh, Mum – is that what the book is all about? A little bit of sunshine on your plate? Why don't you take a break somewhere warm and sunny? You've got loads of cash, and no ties. Go abroad for a bit and live a little. I know I would."

"On my own? Your father would have had a fit."

"You don't have to go alone, and you know it," Amy retorted. "Jane Appleby is always nagging you to visit her in Spain and Auntie Joan spends at least a month golfing in the Canaries. You're not short of offers." Amy looked at her mother sadly. "And Dad's been gone five years now…"

"What if I meet someone?" Barbara replied with a petulant sniff. "What if I decide to stay away and not come back?"

"Mum, if you meet a man and

A robin was hopping towards them

fall in love again, we'd all be delighted for you. Honestly."

"What would your daddy have thought about that, Amy?"

"I don't know, Mum. But I do know he always adored you, even though it may not have felt like it at the end. He would never have wanted you to be lonely and unhappy; I'm very sure of that."

mind off that damn robin at the garden centre. Amy had probably forgotten, it was so long ago now, but Tom, Amy's father, had enjoyed a particular affinity with robins. He had called them all "Chippy" and was such a gentle, patient man that he'd literally had them eating crumbs out of his hand. Barbara had playfully

His sudden illness meant that they'd never had the "if I go first" conversation

Amy's eyes followed the direction of her mother's gaze; a robin was hopping cheekily around underneath the empty table opposite. "Oh, look! The poor little thing must have sneaked in through the sliding doors." She sighed in an exaggerated fashion. "Aaah… he must have needed a bit of company, it's so lonely and cold out there." Amy shot a sneaky glance at her mother, slowly stirring her tea. "It must be a sign. A message to you from Dad to find some warmth and friendship."

"Don't be ridiculous, Amy! The creature's hungry, that's all." A ridge of irritation furrowed Barbara's brow. "All those hormones are wreaking havoc with your imagination, my girl. Some kind of sign, indeed…"

Barbara drove back home the long way; it would take her

chided him for sitting out in the garden all day "doing nothing", but the work always got done, one way or another.

Tom had loved the garden; he would unwind for hours out there, following his week in the office. When he was last to the dinner table, he'd flash that gorgeous grin of his and pretend he'd simply forgotten the time.

Tom forgot most things in the end. It was such a cruel disease, dementia. Cruellest to those who had to watch their loved one becoming more and more distant until they eventually faded away completely. It had happened so quickly, and Tom had been so young. It was a rare form of the disease, apparently, and had taken its grip on the man she loved before they even realised it.

Somehow they'd never had the "if I go first" conversation. Life was so full and busy and vibrant, with children and jobs and the noisy day-to-day stuff that makes the world go round. Barbara had never said that Tom should remarry if something happened to her – and Tom had never raised the subject, either.

If only they had.

By the time the doctor had told her what was wrong with him, Tom had already become cold towards her. Barbara had worried he was having an affair. If only. The disease caused the emotional side of the brain to break down first; loss of empathy and awareness of the way his behaviour hurt her. He still looked completely normal and her mother-in-law had characteristically blamed Barbara for his "moods". Tom's diagnosis took away some of the pain of his enmity towards her, but replaced it with the achingly dark, twisting inevitability of an untimely death. *At least he hadn't realised what was happening,* she thought.

five years before Tom's funeral.

Barbara shook her head quickly; she needed to keep busy and lose herself in some sort of activity. It was the only way. She suddenly remembered her plan; one particular recipe had stuck in her mind from that morning, a fennel, lemon and Parmesan salad. She'd enjoyed something similar on holiday with Tom, a decade or so ago. She simply had to have it that evening with the piece of sea bass that was in the fridge, but she was missing a vital piece of equipment. The recipe called for fine shavings of fennel, so she needed to find the mandolin slicer she had bought at an exhibition many years before. She hadn't seen it for ages, which meant one thing: it must be somewhere in the cupboard under the phone. This particular corner of the house filled Barbara with irrational dread—it needed a jolly good sort-out. Maybe it was time to clear it

There was writing on the back – Tom's writing. She trembled as she read it

But Barbara still felt disloyal and guilty every time she laughed or found pleasure in something. Losing the beautiful spirit of Tom before his body was ready to go had resulted in a lack of closure. Her mourning had really started

out once and for all; a sort of pre-spring clean.

Tugging hesitantly at the cupboard handle, she leapt backwards to avoid the avalanche of detritus that cascaded out. A shoe cleaning kit, broken candles,

Fennel, lemon and parmesan salad...

dried flowers, bits of wrapping paper and, quite spectacularly, a tinkle of broken glass. Cousin Rose's vase. It had been a wedding present, a particularly revolting item that Tom had forbidden her to use. Barbara began to pick the shards up, one by one, and a gentle smile flickered across her lips. Tom would be pleased!

Finding it difficult to be methodical, she peered into the gloom for the mandolin slicer and spotted a ridge of beige plastic right at the back. Found it! She reached in and grabbed an edge between her fingers, turning her face away to avoid any newly dislodged objects.

It came quite easily and, as she got up from her knees in triumph, a flash of colour on the carpet

caught her attention. It was a postcard – one they'd brought back as a souvenir from their last foreign trip. A postcard from Sorrento. Barbara's heart flipped over as she picked it up—it must have been in there for over ten years. For some reason she turned it over, as one would if it had been posted through the door, and the breath caught in the back of her throat. There was writing – Tom's handwriting. She trembled as she read: *Barb, this cupboard is a bloody mess! Shoe cleaning kit fell on my foot. Hurts like hell but I still love you, mucky pup. Wonder how long it will be before you read this? Love and hugs and everything. Forever. Tom.*

Barbara let out a ragged sigh and the second tear of the day dropped onto her wrist. He had even dated it – dear old Tom, so precise. And for a moment she thought she must be seeing things; it couldn't be... She trailed her finger slowly beneath the digits – she wasn't mistaken. It was today's date, ten years earlier.

A spectacular coincidence, obviously, but it left her with an overwhelming feeling of warmth and reassurance. Carefully Barbara put the postcard into her cardigan pocket, brushed herself down and picked up the kettle. She padded gently to the sink, aware of the silence that surrounded her, and flicked on the radio next to the toaster. As she quickly turned towards the tap, a ray of sunshine burst through the kitchen window, filtering through the twiggy stems of an unruly clematis. A flicker of movement drew her eyes to the right, to a broad pair of shoulders clad in an army surplus jumper, holes and all. It was just for a split second – she blinked, and he was gone.

That was my Tom, she thought calmly.

Was it a trick of the light? Or even a figment of her imagination? Maybe. Probably.

A sign of hope

The robin paused beside the first buds of a daffodil – new life after the winter

Barbara opened the back door. Of course, there was no one there but Chippy, chirruping happily towards the back lane from the gatepost.

But the sweet, fruity scent of Arrinmore tobacco hung in the chill air and Barbara smiled as she hugged herself warm. They'd stopped making Tom's favourite baccy six years ago and he'd been hopping mad at the time.

Chippy fluttered down and pecked hopefully in the soil. Barbara followed his progress as he made a fuss like only robins can. He halted by the first yellow buds of a daffodil bursting from the dark soil; new life emerging from the darkness of winter.

Her heart rejoiced; spring was coming and Tom had finally found a way to tell her what she needed to know.

He had let her go with his blessing – and now it was time she did just exactly the same.

FROM THE AUTHOR

"Two children and a rabbit don't leave much free time. Ideas always come when I'm cooking or ironing. So I've burned a few things!"

Lil sat next to me, grumbling

On The Move

Anyone with experience of teenagers will have to smile at this amusing, true-to-life story...

By Paula Palmer

 "Kids, we're leaving in ten minutes," I called up the stairs for what felt like the umpteenth time.

"Nearly ready," Lil called back. I fought the urge to shout, "You said that half an hour ago," and set about loading the suitcases into the car. Discovering that three full-sized cases did not fit in the boot, I picked up the lightest, mine of course, and humped it onto the back seat.

"Mum," Josh yelled, sticking his

waxed, puttied, or muddied head out of his bedroom window, his nose ring glistening in the sun. I cringed, imagining Mark's reaction.

"No more problems, we're leaving," I called, marching purposefully into the house.

"I can't find my iPod," he continued yelling. "I'm not going without it."

"Can't you borrow Lil's?" I asked, in hindsight, naïvely.

"No way! Have you heard what she listens to?" he asked, quite clearly disgusted.

"No worse than yours," I muttered under my breath.

I checked off everything on my list. Good, just one final task: watering the garden so that my neighbour, a sweet elderly widower called Ralph, wouldn't have to bother for a couple of days. For once I blessed the fact that we'd so far endured one of the wettest summers on record – it would make things easier for him.

Lil rushed into the kitchen carrying what remained of her wardrobe. Her outlandish hair was currently dyed a mixture of red and black streaks. Her bottom lip was

now pierced as well as her nose. I was even more concerned by her choice of outfit. Did everything have to be black and look as if it had been through a shredder?

"Mum, I need these as well. Can I have my case back?"

"No, Lil, it's in the car, ready to go," I said firmly, taking the clothes from her and carrying them back upstairs. I knew that if I left it to her she would dump them and they'd need ironing again. When I'd finished putting them away, I knocked on Josh's door.

"Josh, we're leaving." I turned to go but realised I'd had no reply. "Josh," I called again, this time hammering on the door. I checked; the bathroom was empty. I tried his bedroom door.

"I see you found your iPod," I smiled sweetly.

"Mum, don't you knock any more? I could have been naked!" he cried, removing his earphones but making no attempt to move from his bed. I rolled my eyes and ordered him downstairs.

We finally set off after an argument over who would share the back seat with my suitcase.

The car soon rang with the sounds of Radio 2, my choice, of course, and the kids complaining about my driving. Lil had won the argument and was sitting next to me, turning regularly to yell at her younger brother who was apparently kicking her seat.

"Josh, stop that. Lil, try to ignore him," I admonished, a headache forming in my temples.

Mum!" Her pierced nose wrinkled in disgust.

Carefully I negotiated the traffic. It was the school holidays, and the whole of England seemed to have decided to join us on the motorway. The kids tutted intermittently and rolled their eyes in annoyance as the traffic came to an unfortunate, yet inevitable standstill.

"Can't you do something with

"We might not like Mark. Or his kids." Josh was gleefully messing up his hair

By the time we stopped at a service station, they had thankfully both settled down with their respective musical tastes blasting their delicate ears. After a coffee we set off again, Lil making a "quick" call to her boyfriend of two weeks' standing, a charming individual with a penchant for pimped-up cars.

"You'll see him soon enough," I consoled her. "One day you'll probably get married – and then two weeks apart can feel like a gift from heaven."

"No one gets married any more,

your hair?" I asked Lil, eyeing up the bird's nest adorning her head.

The look she gave me was scathing, but I persisted. "Perhaps if you could just comb it, it'll calm down a little. I don't want Mark thinking my children are freaks."

Unkind, but I was becoming nervous. I so wanted everyone to get along.

"Thanks, Mum – that's all I need. I could be permanently traumatised by what you just said," Lil exclaimed, looking me up and down in horror just like her father used to.

Eventually we left the motorway

"Perhaps we won't like Mark. Or his kids," Josh piped up, gleefully messing his own hair up even more.

My heart sank and I muttered secret thanks under my breath that he'd got over his Goth eyeliner phase.

"Have you met his kids yet?" Lil asked, finally bored with her iPod.

"No, but I've seen photos. They look very nice."

"Nice?" she repeated, pretending to stick her fingers down her throat.

"Ugh, they sound tragic!" For once Josh agreed with his sister.

"I've shown Mark photos and he thinks the same of you," I replied, choosing not to admit that the photographs had been a few years old. Despite appearances, they were great kids most of the time – but first impressions count, right?

We'd agreed to break the news after the holiday.

"If we do get on, and I'm nice to Mark's snotty-nosed kids, can we have a dog?" Josh tried, as we crawled to a halt once again. I glanced at the temperature gauge, which was rising, and the petrol gauge, which wasn't. I should have filled up at the service station.

"Maybe," I conceded. It might not be a bad idea. A dog could help bind the two families together.

As we crawled along again, I spotted a sign for our turn-off. Thankfully a petrol station appeared soon after. I filled the tank while Lil and Josh filled a basket with crisps and chocolate, leaving me with a hefty bill but high hopes they would share them

The cottage was a bit small. If the kids didn't get on, this could be disastrous

"Mum, what if we don't get on? Can we leave early? Imagine if we instantly hate each other. We couldn't possibly spend two weeks together, could we?" Lil asked, anxious to get home to Car Boy.

"You won't," I insisted, wondering whether this holiday was such a good idea. Mark and I planned to move in together, but we'd decided the kids should meet in a relaxed, informal way, with no pressures of impending cohabitation to cloud their views.

with Nicola and James, Mark's angelic-looking children.

It was after lunchtime and swelteringly hot when we eventually arrived at the cottage we'd rented for two weeks. It looked charming and the sea views were stunning. Josh loved the fact that the cottage was so old, and learning that there might be a ghost, cheered up immensely. Lil looked less than impressed – until she caught sight of some teenage

The sea views were wonderful

boys on the beach.

There was no sign of Mark, so I let myself in and began unpacking, picking the master bedroom for myself and him. Hmmm, that would be something else for the kids to learn to accept.

The cottage was smaller than I expected. If the kids didn't get on, this could be disastrous – especially as there were only three bedrooms, so the girls would have to share one and the boys another.

I started to prepare lunch and discovered a well-stocked larder in the tiny kitchen. By the time Mark and his kids arrived, I'd prepared a sumptuous spread which we carried out into the garden. We explored the cottage properly and discovered lots of surprises hidden behind doors – including a widescreen television.

That evening we all strolled along the beach and I realised that Mark hadn't even mentioned the kids' piercings or hairstyles. In fact, he chatted happily with them, unfazed by their attempts to goad him about his conservative clothes. I couldn't fail to be impressed by his two children – who, despite their appearances, were as cheeky and as much fun as my own.

"Mum thinks appearances are important," Lil was saying to Mark as they stood skimming pebbles. I cringed in anticipation.

She continued, "She's right, though – and we're just glad you got over your first impressions of Mum. She's not too bad when you get past the middle-aged clothes and practical hairstyle."

I gave her a playful swipe, resolving to go shopping for clothes and steal some of her hair gunk in the morning. A trendy mum – now that *would* embarrass her.

After a while I sat down on a rock. I'd been feeling tired a lot lately, not to mention a little nauseous. Maybe a new puppy wouldn't be the only youngster joining our household…

FROM THE AUTHOR

"Relationships can be much harder when you have more to worry about than just your own foibles scaring your partner off!"

ILLUSTRATIONS: GETTY IMAGES, INGLIS THORBURN

Baby Steps

Sink into this lovely tale of a career girl whose life is changed by a baby – and a craftswoman

By Ann Norman

Things I love… I love my husband, Ben. I love the city. I love the old house we're slowly doing up in the suburbs and I love my job. I buy children's clothes for one of the big stores in town. It's a great job. I travel a lot around Europe and sometimes to the States.

And I think I'm pregnant.

There, I've said it. Does that make it real? I don't feel sick, just in turmoil. I haven't told Ben. I hadn't even told myself, really, until just now.

Like all disasters, you never

I'm having a rare couple of days off at the end of a buying season. I went into the chemist to buy a pregnancy testing kit. The result was a bit iffy. I think my shaking hands had something to do with it. So I've now been in to the surgery to make an appointment to see my doctor tomorrow morning.

Usually when either of us gets a day off we're stripping wallpaper, or hammering happily at our old wreck. Today I can't settle to anything. I pulled a piece of paper off a wall and stood staring at it for five minutes wondering what I'd do if, after tomorrow, a baby was a reality. In the recesses of my mind,

It's not really a disaster – but I have no kind of plans for this. What will I do?

think it could happen to you. The unplanned pregnancy is something you read all about on the problem pages in magazines.

Did I say disaster? I don't think that's really what I think. In fact, I'm finding it difficult to think at all.

I never wanted to juggle a big, demanding career with the important job of raising a family. Now here I am, pregnant (I think), without any kind of plan, or even any background of discussions with Ben other than a kind of

**My idea grew into
a blossoming tree**

make me smile. The only rooms finished are the kitchen and lounge. The rest feels like a building site. And as for the garden…

I have to get out of the house. A bit of suburban retail therapy might help. Unfortunately our shopping centre has the best pram

vague and unspoken agreement about starting a family when we had the house finished.

If I wasn't so anxious, that would

shop in the area, and of course next to it is a first-class toy store. Stifling a groan, I take refuge in the coffee shop. If I shouldn't be drinking strong coffee, this is going to be my last espresso.

All the tables are taken so I go to the stools by the window. In an effort not to look out at the pram shop, my eyes wander to the folk around me. I try not to stare at the old lady on the next stool who is dressed, in spite of the warm day, in a fur coat with no sleeves, a flowery blouse tucked into a tweed skirt and navy socks inside sensible shoes. There is a peculiar

thoughts that circle my brain like Formula One cars on a race track.

"I hope tomorrow will be a good day for you."

I nearly fall off the stool. The old lady has gathered up her book and pencil and is leaning towards me to whisper as she passes.

"Oh… er… thank you. What –"

But she is gone.

Now I've been targeted by an eccentric old woman to receive – what? Is she a witch? Were they spells she was writing down? Is she a psychic, who's just sat there reading my mind? I lose my appetite for espresso.

Who am I to pass judgement on anyone else's rationality, today of all days?

purple felt hat beside her cup and she's writing carefully in an exercise book. My eyes are drawn to the page, and widen when I see that the old lady has already covered it in neat gibberish.

I look away, embarrassed at witnessing an aberration of mental powers in a stranger. Who am I to judge, today of all days, any real inability to behave in a sane and rational manner?

She turns the page and heads the next with a group of random letters, then continues in the same curious code.

I sigh and sip my coffee, drifting off into a reverie of very worried

Ben stares at me, doing his Cheshire-cat impersonation. His big smile is one of the things I love about him. But in this moment, at dinner the next night, I want him to be worried like me. I want him to see my heart banging like a pneumatic drill, not from excitement but from panic.

He drags me to my unsteady feet, crushing me in his arms. "Oh, Amy! A baby! That's wonderful."

Finger under my chin, he lifts my face. His grin vanishes. "I'm sorry." He kisses me gently. "I know you're worried…"

"I'm not worried, I'm panic-stricken. The doctor gave me a

won't be staying on after the seventh month, which is now four weeks away. A love of being pregnant and the idea of motherhood has overtaken panic. Ideas and options for the future have dwindled in inverse proportion to the size of my midriff. I'm resigned to being a full-time mum.

Did I say resigned? Not really. It's an idea I've fallen in love with. But I have to confess there's still a bit of me that knows I'll miss the buzz of my job.

Worries were circling my brain

date… it's eight months away…"

Now he looks worried. "Isn't that perfectly normal?"

"Of course, silly, but what will I do? I won't be able to do my job. I can carry on for a bit –"

"There you are, then. Plenty of time to think about the future. Maybe you could work from home. Everybody's doing that."

Ben's a really bright guy, but sometimes his eternal optimism, which I usually love him for, gets in the way of any kind of common sense whatsoever.

"You know I can't do my job just sitting in front of a computer."

He squeezes me again. "Well, something will turn up."

Of course, it hasn't. We're well into a new season's buying and I've warned my employers I

Just as I am leaving the surgery, glowing with good health, after an ante-natal check-up, the receptionist calls me over. She cheerfully hands a brown paper parcel across the desk.

"Hello, Amy. Molly Roberts left this for you."

"For me? I'm sorry, I don't know any Molly Roberts. You must have the wrong Amy."

The receptionist smiles. "Well, she knows you. She knew your last name and described your red hair."

I take the parcel, which is light and floppy. "Er, thank you." I rack my brains, wondering if I've dropped a scarf or glove in sight of this Molly Roberts.

I sit in the car and undo the parcel. There in the coarse brown paper lies the most exquisite, gossamer-fine white shawl, light as a feather and soft as silk, which I suspect is its main fibre. I hurry back into the surgery.

"Look, I still think you must have the wrong Amy. I can't accept this – even though it's beautiful. Who is this Molly Roberts?"

"She's our cleaning lady."

"But I don't know her."

The receptionist shrugs. And I can feel that someone is waiting behind me now.

"Could I at least go to thank her for all her hard work?"

Obviously needing to get rid of this idiot who can't accept a gift gracefully, the girl replies, "She lives in the left end house of Bedford Terrace."

Then, pointedly to the person behind, "Yes, can I help you?"

Bedford Terrace is three streets away, lined with tiny houses. Molly Roberts's has shining windows and paint in need of repair. I lift up the bright and gleaming brass knocker.

Though the eccentric clothes are different, I recognise immediately the fur-coat-with-no-sleeves lady from the café all those weeks ago. Today she is wearing a long black skirt and cream sweater with a long

waistcoat made from a patchwork of country tweeds.

"Hello, dear." Her greeting is a little hesitant.

Ben would confirm I'm not often at a loss for words. Now I'm dumbstruck, remembering a book of mumbo-jumbo and an interesting demonstration of what appeared to be telepathy. "I… em… hello…"

"Won't you come in? I've just made a pot of tea."

I put one foot gingerly inside the door. "I just came to say thank you very much…"

"Come on into the kitchen."

I follow nervously, expecting to see trappings of the occult, or at least eccentric chaos. But the little house is neat as a pin, if slightly shabby. The kitchen with its quaint,

"But I can't accept this"

old-fashioned cupboards is just completely spotless.

"Sit down." Molly Roberts indicates one of two chairs at the tiny table.

"Look, Mrs Roberts…"

"Call me Molly, please."

"Molly, I came to say thank you for the shawl. But you can't give me something so beautiful and precious. I – I don't know you. I…"

"Anyway," Molly goes on. "I've been seeing you around. I waited, to make sure things were going well. I crochet, you see."

"I'm sorry –?"

"I crochet. I crocheted the shawl. I made it for your baby."

"You made it?"

"Mmm, yes. I crochet things for the people I like."

"But – you don't know me."

"I wanted to make something special and give it to a stranger as a surprise"

She looks at me with twinkling brown eyes. "Let's have a cup of tea and I'll explain."

We sit down with our mugs. "I was behind you in the chemist when you bought the pregnancy test kit. You didn't notice me."

"I… I was particularly distracted that day."

"I know. I saw you later when you came in to make your appointment at the doctor's. I clean there, you know. I could see how worried you were. When I left the café, I wanted to give you a little bit of hope."

I remember the strange feeling I'd got, hearing those few words from a person I perceived as probably mentally unhinged.

"I – thank you."

Molly Roberts is probably getting some similar ideas about my mental stability.

"My dear, I'm sure my family in Australia and my friends are fed up with my offerings. I decided it would be nice to make something rather special and give it to someone as a surprise. You can call it eccentric if you like."

That word. I feel myself colour but Molly doesn't seem to notice.

"But why me?"

"Why not? The day I thought of it was when I saw you in the chemist and doctor's surgery and I decided it was fate."

At last I regain the ability to put more than three words together. "When I saw you in the café, you were – er – writing."

"Yes. I was making up a new pattern for your shawl."

"You made up your own pattern for – for this?" Back to mouth-open mode. By now I'd taken the shawl, now wrapped in tissue paper, out of my bag to return to its loving maker.

"I've been crocheting a long time, Amy."

There is a lump in my throat. "Well, it's the most beautiful thing anyone's ever given me. It's a work of art."

"It's just a shawl. You should see what my friend can do when she wants to."

"Does she crochet as well?"

"No, she knits." Molly gets up. "Back in a mo."

She comes back into the room holding a long waistcoat, knitted in a random patchwork pattern of shapes, and breathtaking autumn shades. Speechless again, I take it in my hands, examining the perfectly crafted fabric and finish.

"I keep it for best. And everyone admires it when I wear it."

"I'm not surprised. It's beautiful. Is it knitted on a machine?"

Molly laughed. "No. She makes her own patterns up, too. And everyone in our little club prefers to work by hand."

"You're in a club?"

"Well, just a group of friends really. We meet every Wednesday. Like an old-fashioned sewing bee, I suppose you could call it."

B en looks at me with his head on one side. "You're going where – to a sewing club?"

"Mmm." I nod happily.

Next day, I'm the one wearing the smug Cheshire Cat-style grin

"You're taking up sewing?"

"No. I'm just thinking something through. And I don't know why I didn't think of it before."

"Are you okay?"

I laugh at the look on his face. "Yes, I'm fine – very fine. I'll tell you all about it tomorrow."

Next day I am the one with the Cheshire Cat-style grin and Ben is frowning. "You mean you're going to rely on a group of elderly women, admittedly with great skills, for the foundation of a new career that you'll run from home?"

"Not exactly. Did you know, smocking is making a comeback?"

"What's smocking? No, don't tell me. Look, Amy, what is it you're going to try to do, exactly?"

I can't really blame Ben for his concern. When I arrived at the crowded house of Molly's friend and saw the work these women did in their spare time, the tiny seed of an idea quickly grew into a full-blown, blossoming tree.

There was Molly's crochet, her friend Babs's knitting, and one of the ladies was doing exquisite embroidery on fine lawn material.

"I'm going to set up a website selling top quality children's clothes. And –" I'm on a roll here – "there'll be a section for expensive, custom-made garments for adult customers, too."

"I remember you saying you couldn't do your job from home."

"I can't buy for stores from home, but I have got more than enough experience of the manufacturers to buy for myself."

"And what are you going to do when your ladies are too old to cope with all the work?"

"There's a resurgence in the old crafts. Younger people are learning them, even at university. That would help to keep us up-to-date in fashions, too."

Ben blinks. "Is there anything I can do to help?"

I think about the boxes, paint and tools in the undecorated room off the kitchen. "Well… I'll need to use the store room as an office."

One gorgeous baby, Molly, and a frantic 12 months later, I am set up. Okay, I might have thought of the website eventually, but it would never have had its exclusive quality without my new friend, and we love the name anyway. After little Molly, the buzz I get from my work and Ben's unstinting support, the thing that has given me the greatest pleasure was the day Molly delivered her first very expensive shawl for despatch. She was wearing a dark red cape that a friend had made from a velvet curtain. She sat with baby Molly on her knee, tears in her eyes.

"I never realised the work could be so valuable. Do you know what you're doing for me, Amy?"

"No, Molly."

She looked up. "You're making it possible for me to go and see my family in Australia. I couldn't afford it before." She dipped her head to kiss baby Molly's soft curls. "I'll be able to see my own great-granddaughter for the first time."

FROM THE AUTHOR

"This was inspired by an encounter my daughter had in a London café, with an old lady who was dressed exactly as described."

Horses Mig

By Angela Lanyon

D o you have to make so much mess, Lee?" Mum looked despairingly at the scatter of cornflakes around his bowl. "You are a trying child! You know I'm in a hurry."

Lee hung his head. He *did* try, but somehow trying at school and trying at home seemed to mean two different things. At six, it was too difficult for him to understand, and now Mum had to go to work every day there was never time for her to explain. He'd left his friends behind when they moved house. Now, it seemed, no one ever had time to notice him.

It was the same when he got to school. He sat clutching a pencil,

Miss stood behind him. "What's the matter this time?"

"It won't go right." Grey eyes met grey eyes above a cat's cradle of pencil marks. Lee hadn't got to grips with making letters, and as for joined-up writing – you might as well expect a horse to fly.

Lee knew what horses were, in a vague sort of way. He'd seen films on the telly about knights on horseback, waving swords and rescuing people. When he'd asked Mum about them she'd just said, "Oh, Lee, not now – I'm trying to make dinner."

Perhaps they were pretend, he thought. Like his writing. The letters were there, or seemed to be, but when Lee looked hard he saw they were only strange and wobbly

All he wanted was to write something, and make Miss and his mum smile

staring through the window while everyone around him was busy writing. With arms and legs uncoordinated, clothes rumpled, hair like windblown thatch and eyes drowning in bewilderment, Lee knew he was a mess.

lines straggling down the page.

"If you spent less time looking out of the window…" Miss began. Her hair was cut very short, and she frowned as she bent over. Lee wished she would smile at him, as she did at the other children. Just

ht Fly

Your heart will go out to
Lee, struggling so hard to
conquer the art of writing

No one seemed
to notice him…

as she looked away, he thought, *Maybe she'll put on her understanding face, like the lady in the paper shop.* The shop lady always shook her head when Lee went in and said what a pity it was about his dad. He knew she felt sorry for him, because sometimes she even gave him an extra penny chew for free.

"Why don't you write about one of your toys?" Miss suggested. "Or is there anything else you like?"

"Horses," Lee said. Miss looked puzzled, so he repeated it.

"Do you know anything about horses, Lee?"

Lee shook his head.

"Have you ever seen a horse? A real horse?"

Lee shook his head again. He didn't tell her about his special dream horse. The one that flew. She'd only laugh.

"So why do you want to write about them?"

"I just do," he said stubbornly.

Sometimes Miss shouted at him, but this time she found a new piece of paper and asked him which horses were his favourites.

"Brown ones, Miss."

"Here, then. *My horse is brown.*" She wrote the words in big letters. "See if you can copy that. I'll find you a crayon, it might be easier for you to hold."

Lee stole a sideways glance at the girl next to him, but she had her arm round her book and put

out her tongue when she saw him peeking. Then he looked at the clean page with Miss's neat writing at the top. It was level. No bits slid down the paper, ending in wavering squiggles.

He touched the letters with his fingers, feeling the slight greasiness of the crayon. He decided the word in the middle must be "horse", although it didn't look like one. He turned the page upside down. It still didn't look like a horse. He tried to copy, eyes locked in concentration, crayon firmly clutched in his hand.

The crayon broke.

It was awful. He was never going to write. Tears trembled on his lashes and he looked round quickly in case any of the other children had noticed. The bigger boys already called him "stupid" and if they saw him crying, they'd call him a cry baby as well. Lee quickly wiped his arm across his face.

Horse. My horse is brown. Lee thought of the films, remembering he'd seen dragons and space ships on the telly as well as knights in armour. Once, in the park, he'd met a man who had really ridden a horse – or said he had. It sounded very exciting.

Then Mum had come and hurried him away. She had shouted, said he must stay close to

It was his special dream horse

brave like his dad. When he tried hard, he could just remember playing football with him in the garden, Mum laughing with excitement when Lee scored a goal. Now they didn't have a garden and since Dad had been killed, Mum never laughed. And so long as Lee was quiet, she didn't seem to notice what he did.

her and not speak to strangers.

"My crayon's broke," Lee said.

Miss wasn't listening. "That's more than enough for this afternoon, everyone," she said. "Put all your things away."

Lee knew she thought he was no good. He wanted to tell her about how difficult writing was, but when he looked up she was helping one of the girls into her coat.

The next day, Miss wasn't at school. She wasn't there the following day, either. The day after that, they had a supply teacher. His name was Mr Walker and he had dark curly hair and a big smile. Lee wondered who supplied him and where he came from. He liked the way Mr Walker strode round the classroom and made silly jokes.

In the morning, Mr Walker let Lee put big seeds into a pot for the sunflowers they were going to grow but when they came back from dinner, he said, "Now we are all going to write some stories."

"Let's see, Lee. You're writing about a horse?" Mr Walker crouched beside him

I'll practise some more when I get home, he thought.

It was a long way down the street. Mum said he was too young to play out on his own, no matter how often he told her he was a big boy now – after all, when he grew up he was going be a soldier and be

Lee felt himself curl up inside. Mr Walker would see at once that he couldn't write and then he'd sigh and stop smiling at him.

"So, Lee, you're writing about a horse?" Mr Walker crouched right down beside him.

Lee hung his head. "I'm not

much good at writing," he began to mumble under his breath.

He couldn't bring himself to say that he couldn't write at all.

"Tell me about the horse," Mr Walker said. There was something about Mr Walker; Lee could feel him listening. So he told him all about the dragons and unicorns we'll pin them on the wall so that your mums and dads can see them when they come round to parents' night this evening."

Lee had forgotten it was parents' evening. Everyone else would be ooh-ing and aah-ing, but he'd have nothing to show. His mum would say, "Never mind," but he knew she

"My goodness!" said Mum, seeing his work on the wall. "Aren't you clever?"

and the knights who rode about rescuing people, and explained that when he grew up he was going to rescue people too.

Eventually, at last, in a voice hardly above a whisper, he told Mr Walker about his flying horse.

To his great surprise, Mr Walker knew all about the flying horse. He called him Pegasus, and in the Literacy Hour when they listened to stories, he told the whole class all about him. Only he didn't let on about Lee.

Waking up the following morning, Lee felt sick. Suppose Mr Walker had gone away? But when he got to school, there he was, standing behind his desk with a pile of coloured paper and crayons and scissors.

"We are going to write our stories on all sorts of paper and in lots of different colours," he told the class. "When you've finished,

would be disappointed. He blinked, and decided he was going to try very hard.

He chose a brown pencil and rough, brown paper, almost the colour of his dad's uniform, but

At last, he had something to show!

when he tried to write on it, it slid off the table. Every time he moved his arm the paper moved, too.

"Can I cut out, Mr Walker?" he asked. Anything was better than trying to make letters.

Mr Walker gave him a pair of scissors and Lee bent over the table. If he spent the morning cutting out paper, no one would notice he hadn't written anything. He started to snip away at a new, white piece of paper. Small pieces, like bites in a biscuit. Then they got smaller. Slowly, he found a horse was happening. Not a flying horse, or even a galloping horse, but a sort of solid one with square legs and round tummy and a spiky tail that stuck out behind. With great care he drew an eye.

"Well done, Lee. What a splendid horse." Mr Walker must have been watching him all the time after all. "What's his name?"

He's Pegasus, can't he see? Bitterly, Lee knew why the teacher had asked. It wasn't a splendid horse; it was just a piece of white paper.

"It's Pegasus, isn't it?" Mr Walker was saying. "Why don't you write it down, and then everyone will know." He wrote "My horse is Pegasus" in Lee's book and left him with a sheet of blue paper to copy it on to.

Lee bent over his table and stared at the writing. This was his horse; not anyone else's.

My horse is Pegasus.

It took him a long time, and when he had finished his hands were damp, his face shining and his shoulders cramped with effort. But he had written. He had written words. Words that his mother could read.

"My goodness!" Mum said that evening, when she saw his horse on the classroom wall. "Aren't you clever!"

"Amazing," agreed Mr Walker, though he didn't seem to be looking at the horse but right at Lee's mum.

"Pegasus," his mum said. "That's a funny name for a horse."

"It's a very special horse," Mr Walker said. "You'll have to get Lee to explain."

"It's sort of magic…" Lee began. Then he looked up and saw a smile beginning on Mum's face, and Mr Walker grinning at her like crazy.

Maybe Pegasus really was a magic horse, after all. He hoped so.

FROM THE AUTHOR

"When I'm not being a grandmother and writing stories, I love writing murder mysteries for the amateur stage."

One Moment Of Madness

We all hide secrets about our past, but when the memories haunt us, they can be hard to escape…

By Rose Layland

There's a fascination about heights." Hannah had been mildly pleased that the ascent of the tower had made her only slightly breathless, although she'd not wanted to admit to her now aching calf muscles.

"I think we can see our house." Her husband gazed about the circular view with interest.

"You feel drawn to the edge, and there's almost a compulsion to jump."

seconds to live. To jump or not to jump, that is the question…"

"Bit extreme, aren't you?" John stared at her quizzically, but was soon away again, finding landmarks, identifying familiar places from an unusual angle.

"It's the same going over a high railway bridge, wondering if it's going to hold. Relief when the train reaches the other side."

"That's Rollard's Industrial Unit. I can count their vans."

"But an ideal murder." Hannah murmured on. "Unless there's a

"Did they jump or were they pushed? Was it an accident? Suicide?"

"Yes – see?" He pointed. "The poplar. Just to the right. The one with the shed."

"I expect it crosses everyone's mind," Hannah continued. "What it would be like with all that space under you. Knowing you only had

struggle, of course, that might leave marks. But otherwise, who's to say? Did they jump or were they pushed? Was it an accident? Suicide? Unless there's a witness, there's no proof."

She hadn't been up here for 40

Hannah could see the tower from her bedroom

years, but she'd often stared at the tower from her bedroom window. Grey, castellated, it had pierced the centuries impassively. Seen much more than a falling figure. Henry VIII's impassioned scourges, and Cromwell's, too. It was said that the sad remnants of some of Monmouth's rebels were buried beside the little south door.

Beside a history of war and turmoil, the death of a fourteen-year-old girl was of little account. And although there was a tablet set beside the foot of the tower recording the event, it was now rarely noticed: a forgotten incident in a small town's past.

Cynthia Radley had been the headmistress's daughter, and a right little madam she'd been, too. A proper bully. A tyrant in the playground. She had about her the arrogance of power.

To be sent to Coventry by Cynthia and her cronies was an abyss of misery; to be included in her playground activities, the pinnacle of relief and happiness. Her delight was to torment, to manipulate and to humiliate. And she'd sharpened these weapons on Hannah. She had it all off to a tee. How to make much of the younger girl, draw her into the privileged inner circle and then to cut her off with the suddenness of a knife,

being sick." But a few moments later, for once, they had been alone together. Cynthia was never at her best alone. She liked an audience, and the reinforcement of a gang. But the others had gone down, lured, no doubt, by the prospect of a cream tea, laid on by the church for this school visit as part of a history lesson.

The bells had begun to boom. They'd even got the ringers in to make more of an occasion. There could be felt the alarming sensation of the tower beginning to sway under the influence of the swinging tons of bronze.

"Ooooaaah" Cynthia clutched the parapet castellations. It was the

The fear visible in her face triggered an uncontrollable urge for revenge

humiliating and isolating her in front of a host of grinning friends.

The playground could be a lonely place. Hannah, with her sweet, but unsure disposition, and her inclination to see the best in people, became Cynthia's victim again, and again, and again.

She put her hand each side of the castellations. This was where it had happened. Almost timidly, she looked over. The gargoyle, with its protruding tongue, was still there.

"Look," Cynthia had called, gesturing downwards and inviting her sycophants to laugh. "Hannah

first time Hannah had ever seen her show signs of being out of control. The expression of fear in her face triggered an uncontrollable urge for revenge. From then on, it were as though everything that happened had been done by someone else, as though Hannah had watched someone else cross swiftly and knock Cynthia's hands off the stones, lift and push her backwards off her feet. The deafening clanging of the bells drowned her screams. It was as though someone else had descended the

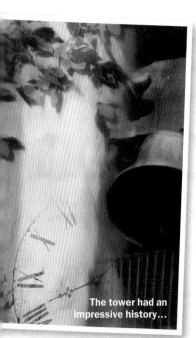

The tower had an impressive history…

for the small, narrow door which gave to the stairs. Hannah giggled as they made their way cautiously down the spiralling steps. She put her mouth to his ear on the turn.

"I don't think we're supposed to be up here when they ring the bells!"

They took their cream teas round to the foot of the tower and sat on a bench.

"Haven't seen that before." John, scone in hand, was reading the tablet set outside the tower. He looked upwards. "Poor kid."

The bells began to vibrate in Hannah's head, awakening a maelstrom of memories.

"She deserved it." she cried savagely. John glanced at her in disbelief. "I went to school with her. She was a vindictive bully. She tried to destroy me."

"Even so…" John was struggling with the change in his wife.

"I did it! There was triumphant and reckless venom in her cry. "And no one ever suspected…"

John's disbelieving gaze was focused behind her. The vicar had heard it all.

And the bells crashed on…

stairs and joined the others without attracting attention. It was a quarter of an hour before the body was found. Hannah had thought about it a lot during the weeks and months which followed, but as time went on, the whole thing had taken on the vagueness of a bad dream. She'd been married at the church, attended services sporadically, and now lived within sight of the tower. She'd come to a time when she could look at it without remembering at all. Now the bells began their deep-throated notes and the tower began to sway.

"Ow." John gave her an alarmed grimace, caught her hand and made

ILLUSTRATIONS: MANDY MURRAY

FROM THE AUTHOR

"I was horrified to find when I stood once on a church tower, that it moved when the bells rung. It was the oddest feeling."

Callisto being pursued by the Greek god Zeus, twisting a scrap of tear-dampened linen between slender fingers. She had lived the myth, by all accounts; sold into marriage to a cruel man, with none but his unmarried elder sister brave enough to protect her from the force of his fists and tongue.

Lady Emma sat beside her now, ready to offer a comforting embrace if need be. It was rumoured she'd been given until the end of the year to find a husband, or else accept the veil at St Benedict's sister abbey, as the penny-pinching Warin had already tired of feeding and clothing her.

enough to have shot straight, had I intended to step straight into Warin's boots."

Gilbert wondered what in his expression had prompted the other man's defence.

"Well, in my medical opinion," he said quietly, "your aim was not the reason you are now Lord of Fulbrooke. Did Sir Warin eat or drink anything today that could have been tainted in any way, perhaps even poisoned?"

There was a stunned silence.

"Why would you ask?" Lady Emma enquired in the echo of Helena's strangled gasp.

"You sewed the arrow wound

"Brother Gilbert looks to entertain us with tales of poison." His voice cracked

She was no beauty, Gilbert mused, but a calm, unassuming woman with an understated intellect, a talent for healing, and gifted at plying her needle. It was her work that adorned the walls of the solar and the great hall below. Better attributes for a wife to possess than looks, he would have thought. There was no accounting for taste, though.

He cleared his throat. "My lord."

Simon started at the unfamiliar address, then sat up and blinked at the monk. "I know my sight is not as strong as yours, Brother," he said trenchantly. "But it is good

Lotions and potions...

yourself, my lady; it wasn't severe enough to cause rapid death. With the stomach sickness and breathing difficulties that I was too late to treat, I would say the patient imbibed something poisonous either by accident, or indeed, otherwise."

Helena buried her face in her hands. Emma rose.

"Excuse us, gentlemen. My lady is in shock and needs to rest."

She led the wilting young woman from the solar, passing Fulbrooke's steward entering. He was a tall man, with a serious face and a steadfast reputation.

"Hugh," Simon greeted him in a cracked voice. "Brother

Gilbert looks to try to entertain us with tales of poison."

Hugh's eyes popped; he shot a very worried look at the monk.

"What?" Simon scoffed. "You doubt, too?"

"I saw the wound," Hugh confessed. "It seemed little more than a scratch."

"With your permission, my lord," Gilbert interrupted. "I would like to examine that arrow."

The steward insisted on accompanying Gilbert to the chapel, where Lord Warin's body lay in state.

"Few folk will mourn the man," Hugh told the monk bluntly. "But it would be better for my lord Simon's future if he were not accused of murder!"

"You have served this manor for some years now, have you not?" asked Gilbert.

"Over half my lifetime. I love Fulbrooke, despite the unhappiness here of late."

"And, therefore, you would do all you could to protect the family, even a tyrant like Lord Warin?" At Hugh's look, Gilbert shrugged. "We monks are sequestered from the world, sir, not dead to it."

"Warin was a devil," Hugh admitted. "Impatient with his tenants, insulting to his family. Let us say it will be no hardship to serve Lord Simon instead, though he's no soldier."

"You think Simon might have hankered after Fulbrooke?"

"Not in the way you're implying. And that a poisoned arrow would prove his guilt is ridiculous. Anyone could have infected the tip – even the fletcher who forged it."

"But none," Gilbert murmured, "with quite so much to gain."

"Only a cloistered monk could think that inheriting mismanaged estates was a gain."

"Perhaps," conceded Gilbert with a bow of his head. "Yet all men still pray for them."

The chapel was silent, the dark-robed lord's corpse untouched, and the arrow nowhere to be found. Gilbert had a feeling that even had it still been here, it would be wiped clean.

The bailey had a well-tended physic garden that Brother Gilbert had visited in the past, when called on to care for the demesne's sick and dying souls. Upon entering, he saw Lady Helena kneeling amongst the flowers, methodically sorting and collecting blooms. Tucking his hands into the sleeves of his cloak, Gilbert approached tentatively, noting fresh tear stains on my lady's porcelain cheeks. She looked so young, yet a life of worry was already worn into her features.

The garden was a soothing place

"Those are pretty," he said kindly, gesturing to her posy as he sank onto a narrow bench against the wall.

"It is Emma who knows what to pick and dry for food and medicine," Helena replied self-consciously. "I merely help her sometimes in her task; the garden is so soothing."

And the one place the brutish Warin was unlikely to visit, Gilbert thought shrewdly.

"You look flushed, my lady," he observed. "Are you well?"

Helena tugged nervously at the woollen shift lying high across her shoulders. It was too warm a robe

her life, and mine." A flush crept up her neck. "I am expecting again, and Warin swore, were it not an heir this time, he'd kill me with his bare hands. I've been praying, but…" Glancing at the band digging into her finger, she finished poignantly, "Sometimes God doesn't hear."

Gilbert watched her as she absentmindedly shredded the flowers that were lying in her lap.

"Did you see what my lord ate today, or who served him?"

Her sooty eyes rose immediately to meet the monk's.

"I served him, from the trencher we shared. Had it been infected, then I would surely have died, too." She blinked. "God moves in mysterious ways, brother; is that not what you say?"

Before Gilbert could reply, Lady Emma appeared in the garden, carrying a tiny curly-haired child. Helena jumped up, sending the flowers flying, and joyfully held out her arms.

"Mary, my heart! Excuse me,

for June, but Gilbert suddenly guessed why she had worn such a concealing garment and felt a pang of sympathy.

"Lord Warin was not a gentle man, I'm told."

"No," Helena murmured. "Not

"No," Helena murmured, her hand at her throat. "He was not gentle"

gentle, or patient." Her hand stole to her throat. "I have lived in fear of saying or doing wrong, of angering him. He had no kindness for anyone, not even his own daughter. I feared sometimes for

Brother Gilbert. I must put my daughter to bed."

Gilbert rose to bow to her, slowly re-seating himself as he watched mother and child walk away. At his inviting gesture, Lady

Emma came to sit beside him. She, too, looked after Helena with a wistfulness that he had not seen in her before.

"So, old mare," he said, referring to the insult Lord Warin had often dealt his sister in public. "I wanted to thank you for your help in tending to your brother earlier. It cannot have been easy."

Emma nodded. "I've learned what I can over time," she said in her measured way. "If I wasn't destined to be of benefit to a family of my own, I was determined to do what I could to help those around me."

"Will you still look to join our sister abbey at year's end?"

"Most likely. Warin believed that such a life would be abhorrent to

There was much to be said for remaining unmarried

"My work here is also done," Emma replied. "She and the children are safe"

me, and I was content to let him think it if it meant he let me be. My only regret is not having a child of my own to love and care for. But one need only look at poor Helena to see there is much to be said for remaining unmarried."

"Amen to that," Gilbert said in agreement, thinking of my lady's well covered bruises.

It was a humid night, not ideal for sleeping, even had Gilbert's mind quietened enough for him to seek rest. Instead, he wandered the buildings and boundaries of the manor, puzzling over its inhabitants. Last night their lord had been a cruel and callous tyrant; this morning, a reasonable scholar. He could already feel a change in the air – a whispering hope, a butterfly finally emerging from its chrysalis.

Yesterday's events whirled through his mind, struggling to piece themselves together into a satisfactory conclusion.

Fulbrooke's overpowering presence had caused so much strife here that brother, sister, tenants and wife all had a motive to remove it. But perhaps he had been wrong about poison. Perhaps, quite simply, Lady Helena was correct about God's mysterious ways and Lord Warin had simply endured one wound too many eventually.

Despite the early warmth without, the women's bower on the first floor of the keep was blessedly cool, inhabited at this hour only by the Lady Emma.

Gilbert observed her in silence for a moment as she deftly wove her needle in and out of a large tapestry loom, bringing the cloth to life.

"Good morrow, brother," she said without looking up. "You wish to see me?"

"Merely to bid you farewell," Gilbert answered. "My work here is done. Perhaps I shall see you in the abbey one day, mistress. I suspect, though, that life at Fulbrooke will now be much changed, and Lady Helena is sure to want you to remain as her guardian, especially with another baby on the way."

Emma paused.

"My work here is also done," she said. "She and the children are safe now. I know Simon will ensure they and the manor are well taken care of. And I would live out the rest of my life now in repentance of my sins."

"That salve you used to staunch my lord's blood before you stitched the wound," Gilbert ventured. "With what did you make it?"

Emma turned slowly with a sad and wistful half-smile.

"A prayer and a potent liquid of crushed stems, Brother Gilbert. But there is none left and I will not give you the recipe. I am certain that your own remedies are much more efficacious."

Gilbert sighed.

"I think I understand now," he said softly. "With that protective nature, you would have made a good mother, old mare."

Then, raising his hood over his tonsured head, he left the bower, relieved to return to the peace of his priory.

For a long moment, Lady Emma stared after him. Then she turned and with a slow, steadying breath, began once again to ply her needle.

FROM THE AUTHOR

"History and how people really lived is a fascinating subject. This tale gave me the chance to delve into both aspects."

Fairground Attraction

What could be more romantic than being swept off your feet by the lovely man on the waltzers?

By Linda Mitchelmore

A ugust, hot and sultry – the wicked month – and Becky is glaring at me. "Helen, have you gone mad?" she yells at me over the noise of the fairground. "You must have been on the waltzers at least five times now!"

"Seven," I reply, holding out the appropriate number of fingers towards her. "And I'll go on the ride just as many times as I want to."

remember just about everything.

It's been a tradition for years that Becky and I meet up on the first night of the fair. We haven't missed a first night yet – not even the year Becky gave birth to her first child two weeks before.

Me? I've never married. There was never anyone who fired that spark in me – a spark that would turn into a fast burn. But there is now. I have always said I'd know my soulmate when I met him – and now I have. And he's beckoning to

I'd always said I'd know my soulmate as soon as I met him. And there he was

"You'll be sick with that constant spinning around. Just remember how sick you used to get riding the umbrella swing in the park?"

That's the trouble with being out with the best friend you've known since you were five – they can

me from the waltzers, which have just stopped to change customers.

He waves at me and I give a little wave back. He's wearing a white T-shirt tucked into very faded jeans and looks like he works out, although I imagine spinning the

It feels so right
to be with him

waltzers around for hours each day would give anyone toned arms and a six-pack. His hair is neither brown nor black, but somewhere in between; shorter than blokes wear their hair these days. He looks arty, almost – not like the usual bloke you get working at the fair.

And his eyes are green, like sage leaves. I don't think I'll ever forget those eyes, or the way they did a double-take the first time I climbed into a waltzer.

I don't even know his name yet, but I feel there's definitely a bit of a connection between us.

"Oh, you have to be kidding me," marriage, babies and all that."

"Who said anything about marriage? I don't even know his name yet. But I will."

I'm talking to Becky, but my eyes are searching him out over the heads of the people clambering on to the ride. I'm going to have to go soon. And I think Becky has already sensed my determination.

"I'll be over at the Inn on the Green when you've come to your senses. But if you don't I'll be leaving at 10pm."

"Okay," I say. "I'll make this up to you, but I've got a feeling in my

We look shyly at one another, like two kids who don't know the dating game

Becky says, horrified. She's just noticed why I keep returning.

"You've never gone and fallen head-over-heels for someone who works the fair circuit?"

"Might have," I say coyly.

"Well then, you'd better un-'might', PDQ. Come on," Becky says grabbing my arm. "I'm going to get you a cup of very strong coffee and you're going to listen to me while I tell you this is not a good idea. He'll be leaving at the end of the week…"

"I'm not going anywhere but on that waltzer," I tell her firmly

"But you're a career girl, Hels," Becky pleads. "You don't do

insides like nothing I've ever had before. And if I don't see it through, I truly think I might regret it for all time."

I give Becky a hug. "Be careful, that's all." She shrugs.

"I will," I say, but I'm already walking away, distracted.

"Hi," he says as I slip my hand into his outstretched one and he helps me on to the seat.

He pulls the bar up to secure me in place. Just me. He's not letting anyone else in this cubicle.

"Hi," I reply. I offer him my £2 coin for the ride but he firmly shakes his head.

"Let's get away from the noise"

"I'm due a break after this ride. We could walk over to the pier, get away from the noise. Yes?"

I nod. He's just said the things I was hoping he'd say.

The waltzers begin to move. I feel a shock of something as his hand brushes across the top of my head – it could be static electricity from the ride, but I don't think so.

"Speed-dating doesn't come close, does it?" he jokes as, at last, the ride slows down, stops, and we leave together.

We look at one another like kids who don't know the dating game – to hold hands or not; link arms or not; walk close and accidentally touch? And we laugh, as though we are both thinking the same thing.

In the end we settle, unspoken, for the latter option as we walk away from the fair together.

The café on the end of the pier is practically empty of customers. It's quiet in here behind the double glazing. He puts a hand in the small of my back, the gentlest of touches, and gently guides me to a table by the window. The lights on the prom have just come on. They look like necklaces of pale blue, solar-powered globes.

"You look like a black-coffee sort of woman to me… er…" He guesses at my preference.

"Helen. And I am." I wonder for a moment what it is he thinks a black-coffee woman looks like, but decide not to ask. "And you?"

"Alex. I take my coffee black, too. So we've got something in common already."

He tips his head on one side and smiles at me and my insides turn to melting marshmallow. Then we do the formal handshake thing smiling idiotically at one another and Alex goes to fetch our drinks. And I will my insides – and my head and my heart – to return to some sort of adult normality.

"So," he asks, plonking two mugs of coffee and a single KitKat – how does he know they are my weakness? – on the table between us. "Local? Holidaymaker? Other?"

"Local," I tell him. "I teach – learning support."

"And it's never left a lot of time for anything else?" He's looking at my ring-finger hand.

"Until now, no," I tell him. "And what about you?"

"Divorced. My ex-wife didn't like what I do."

He waves a hand towards the flashing lights of the fairground. Then he unwraps the KitKat and separates the bars, handing me one of them.

"As you've seen, I'm working the waltzers at the moment."

"Just 'til the end of the week?"

"Just until then," he says. "But do you think we could get to know one another a little better in the little time we have?"

"A holiday romance?" I smile.

Already I feel sad that that's all it might be, but I know it will be better than not getting to know Alex – and who knows, if we give it a chance, it might turn into something we both want.

"Although neither of us is on holiday, are we?" Alex points out.

"We're not. No time to waste, then," I declare.

So we don't. We hold hands as if it is the most natural thing in the world to do as we walk the length of the promenade to the harbour and back again.

Alex asks about my work, and I tell him. I still get a thrill, seeing children who aren't expected to achieve – well, achieving. Seeing the delight on their faces as they read three words in a row for the first time, or triumphantly realising that two and two equals four.

"I can't imagine not being able to read, can you?" Alex remarks.

"Imagine never being able to read Dickens, or Shakespeare."

I hadn't expected him to say that, and I'm cross with myself for pigeon-holing him just because he works the fair.

"Or Anita Shreve, or Edna O'Brien, or P. D. James?"

"Especially P. D. James," Alex says, smiling down at me.

"Crime's my thing too," I say. "A. J. Newson? Ever read him?"

"Every word," he says with a grin. "Another thing we have in common, Helen."

Alex drops my hand as a couple comes towards us and we walk – his hand on my shoulder guiding me away from the edge of the promenade – one behind the other, to let them pass. But he keeps his hand on my shoulder afterwards and that feels right too.

"Shouldn't you be getting back to the waltzers?" I ask.

"Nope. Not tonight. I've already

I'm caught up in a whirl of feelings

squared it with the big boss."

"So, where do you go in the winter time?"

"I have a bit of a bolt hole."

I don't ask where that is because it might be a long way from here.

We seem to be walking slower and slower as though we don't want the night to end. The lights of

those would be the only words I'd want to hear."

For the rest of the fair week Alex and I meet during the day – school's out for now and, while I've got lessons for the new term to plan, I know I can get them done in time for the latest lot of students.

Behaving like holidaymakers, we stroll along the cliff path, stopping to kiss

the fairground are starting to go off one by one, and slowly people begin to leave.

"After my divorce I didn't date anyone for ages," Alex explains. "And when I did it was disastrous."

I don't know what to say, but eventually I murmur, "I hope I won't fall into the same category."

Alex laughs. "I shouldn't think so. It was fairly dramatic, wasn't it – that bolt of something electric that connected us back there? When was that? – all of three hours ago?"

I look at my watch under a streetlamp. "Five," I tell him.

"Then I'd better walk you home now." So he does.

"I never thought I'd hear myself saying this," Alex says as we stand on my doorstep, not holding hands now, but close. "But do you think I can see you again?"

"And I never thought that

Neither of us has a car. I don't really need one because the school where I work is ten minutes' walk from my cottage. And if I want to go further afield I take the train, or the bus, and sometimes a taxi. And Alex says that doing what he does means he doesn't need a car either.

I'm enjoying showing Alex around my patch. We behave like holidaymakers and take buses and get off where the fancy takes us, walking back along the cliff path, stopping to eat the lunch I've packed. Stopping to kiss.

And we buy ice-cream from the kiosk on the seafront and share it as we stroll along the beach, the sand warm and gritty between our toes. Sometimes we paddle, jumping back as small waves ripple and break on the shoreline, splashing our clothes.

While Alex works his shift at the fair, I stay at home catching up on the things I didn't do in the day when I was with him. Then I pitch up just in time to catch the last ride on the waltzers.

This is a magical time for both of us, and as the time nears for the fair to pack up and leave, I know I don't want what we have between us to ever end.

Today is the last day, and I know that tomorrow when I walk along the promenade, the fair will have already left as though spirited away in the night by some unseen hand. All that will remain will be patches of the palest green where

His kiss comes straight from his soul

I see him, leaning against the wooden wall of the pier café. Why hasn't he left?

the rides and the booths and the tents have been.

"So," Alex says, as we walk together towards the beach, towards the blackness of the night-time sea, "are you going to run away with the fair?"

I gulp. I've been dreading this question for all this time now.

"The sixteen-year-old me would have done," I say. He can make of that what he will.

"But the forty-two-year-old you is more cautious?"

"Much more cautious," I say.

"It's all happened so fast between us, hasn't it?" Alex muses. "Too fast?"

I shake my head, too full up to speak. It's been good. I just can't

bear the thought of not seeing him any more.

And the kiss he gives me then is like no other I've ever had. It seems to come from his soul, straight into mine.

It's just after seven in the morning. I thought I'd kiss Alex goodbye just one more time, but I'm too late and the fair has already left. From here I can see the patches of pale green where it's been – like a random patchwork. It gives me an idea I can try with the children next term. See, already my fractured heart is mending.

Who am I kidding? This hurts like hell; like having vinegar poured on an open wound.

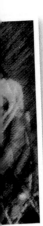

And then I see him. He's leaning against the wooden wall of the pier café. I wonder how long he's been there watching me – and why he is there watching me. Why he hasn't left.

I begin to walk towards him at the exact moment he starts to walk towards me.

"You haven't left with the fair," I say.

"Seems not."

"But how did you know I'd come to… you know…?"

"I knew you'd come sometime. I wanted to be here when you did."

"Well, I…" I say, but Alex stops me and kisses me instead. It is not the sort of sexy kiss that leads to other things, but the sort of kiss that's full of deep and meaningful love all the same.

"I haven't been straight with you," Alex says.

I shiver. Whatever it is he's going to tell me, I don't think I want to hear it. But I have to.

"Go on," I whisper.

"A. J. Newson? Ever heard of him?" he says.

"You know I have," I say. He's talking in riddles and… Oh! I get it. "A for Alex – *you're* A. J. Newson?"

"I'm guilty as charged. I didn't intend to deceive you about what I do but I had to be absolutely certain you felt the same about me as I do about you before I revealed all the facts."

"And are you sure now?" I ask, kissing him.

"Well, that sort of proves it." He laughs as we pull apart, oh, about five minutes later.

"And you worked at the fair for background research for your next book? And for *Bad Feelings* you worked in a car factory? *Dead Notes Falling* meant you learned to play the saxophone?"

"Yep, yep, and yep," he agrees. "And all the others."

"No wonder the settings in your books are so real!"

I don't know where it is his bolt hole is yet, but it doesn't seem to matter right now. I don't think he'll be going back there for quite some time to come.

"The Boathouse does a great breakfast," I say, pulling him along with me in that direction.

"Lead me to it."

"*Sinister Sailing?*" I quip.

"Nope. I'm thinking of changing genre. Romance."

"Romance?" I echo, pulling him close to me. "I think I just might be able to help with some of your research there."

FROM THE AUTHOR

"When the fair arrives with all its noise and smells, I often meet people from my schooldays. This idea came as I walked round this year."

Our Rainbo Fridays

You'll enjoy sharing this touching and tender meeting as we join this loving couple on their long-awaited tryst…

By Linda Finlay

The last Friday of the month. The day I've longed for; the one that has taken forever to come. Even now, at this late hour, I know the phone could still ring, cancelling our precious time together. Even if all does go according to plan, the hours will fly by seemingly in a blink, for it's the that age-old sign of hope, the rainbow. The sunshine after the showers – although, in our case, it's the sunshine between the downpours, when every second is colourful, each moment savoured and treasured

My heart somersaults as I see him draw up and then flips over when he appears

only day of the month we have the opportunity to hopefully cast aside the responsibilities and needs of others and take some time out to concentrate on ourselves.

It is because these times are so precious that we name them after before being consigned to memory. For it's these cherished reminiscences that will sustain me through the dark days that will surely follow. These dark, difficult days that have now come to represent my life.

Bittersweet

We must pace ourselves

I watch from my vantage point and my heart somersaults as his car draws up. He climbs out, all long limbs and floppy dark hair that lifts in the cool breeze of a late spring afternoon. He hurries towards the entrance, clutching a box bound with red ribbon and looking boyishly eager. Only the lines around his eyes betray the strains and stresses of the last months. Despite everything, he's still a very handsome man and my heart tumbles over in another crazy flip of excitement.

As I wait for him, I cast a final glance around the room. Logs crackle their welcome from the fireplace. The table is set for two in the alcove. Crystal glasses glisten in the flickering light of the candles, the warmth of the room releasing the fragrance of my carefully arranged freesias to softly permeate the air. They were a silly extravagance, really, for we only have tonight. That's why it's important that everything is perfect – that I have created the right ambience. Special yet cosy, intimate and yet relaxing.

I flick a switch and the haunting strains of Katie Melua's lovely song *Spellbound* softly fill the room. The intercom buzzes, and I smile – for, although I gave him a key some time ago, he still seeks permission to enter. It's part of our game, you see.

"Hello, sweetheart." He smiles his cheeky welcome and gives me a long, lingering look. It's the intimate look I like to believe is for me alone. He holds out a box of my favourite chocolates, then his lips come down on mine, hungry and full of promise.

As I lean into him, savouring his warmth and the spicy smell of his aftershave, his arms tighten around me and we are together in our own adult world at last. A month's pent-up emotions bubble to the surface as we stand locked

He has my favourite chocolates

in each other's arms, lost in the wonderment of being together, alone. Reluctantly, we pull apart, knowing from experience that we need to slow down the pace, savour each moment, take our time and anticipate.

"You look gorgeous." His eyes soften to melting amber as his glance rakes over me, taking in my shiny auburn hair, carefully-applied make-up and the red flowing dress that clings to my now slender curves. I've worn it because I know it's his favourite and such a contrast to my customary, everyday attire, which through sheer necessity is casual and washable.

Firmly, I quash these thoughts. Nothing must be allowed to encroach upon our special time together. Eager to continue the game, I twirl around in front of him, feeling womanly and thoroughly desirable again.

"Why, thank you, sir." I dip a pretend curtsey. He laughs his rich throaty laugh and I'm instantly transported back to happier times. However, this is now, and I force myself to stay in the present.

"Let me get you a drink. There's wine chilling – or I can make a cup of tea, if you prefer?"

"Wine would be wonderful, but I'll grab a shower first… if you don't mind waiting a little while."

much the extravagance has cut into his meagre allowance.

I cross the room and cosy into the velour sofa by the fire to wait. Waiting – I do a lot of that these days, I muse, then take a sip of my drink, my first for a month. Once, it was wine every Friday night, a reward for the labours of the week when we could relax and responsibilities, such as they were, could be cast aside until Monday morning. Things are different now.

I take another sip, rolling the liquid around my tongue and appreciating its crisp, dry taste. The logs are burning brightly and, as I watch the flames jumping and dancing, I feel an urge to jump and dance, too. Then I realise the water in the shower has stopped running and my heart leaps instead.

I do a lot of waiting these days, but this time I know it will be well worth it

I smile and nod, understanding perfectly. The silk robe he leaves here is already laid out on the bed. He gives me another kiss before disappearing into the bathroom.

Carefully, I pour two glasses, suddenly wishing I'd splurged on champagne. I shake my head at such fanciful thoughts. There's no money for such luxuries these days. My eyes stray to the box of expensive chocolates and I feel warm inside, knowing just how

He appears a few moments later, smiling and smoothing down his damp hair with one hand while carefully placing his mobile phone on the coffee table with the other. I stare at it, willing her not to ring. Although, of course, if it wasn't for her, we couldn't be here – and I am grateful, truly I am. It's just that I've looked forward to tonight so much and, if I'm honest, it has been the only thing that's kept me going during the difficult times of the past month. I couldn't bear it if she had to ring and interrupt our evening together.

He intercepts my look. "It will be fine." He bends forward, kissing me tenderly on the forehead. He smells fresh and invigorating, like a garden after warm summer rain.

I want to take his hand and run off into the darkening night where we can hide and be alone forever. Shaking my head to dispel the

He smiles, then hands me my drink. We chink glasses and pretend. Pretend that we can live our life as other couples do. I look at him and see my burning desire reciprocated in the smouldering warmth of his eyes.

"Are you hungry?" I ask and we laugh, breaking the tension.

"That's an understatement, but let's have food first. A man must have some sustenance," he jokes.

I know we have to be strong for each other... We couldn't cope, otherwise

image, I pull him down beside me instead. "Good choice of music," he murmurs, tucking a strand of hair behind my ear and nibbling my neck.

I sigh ruefully; the track has switched to Norah Jones's *Come Away With Me*. I wish. His kisses reach the low neckline of my dress and desire wells up inside me like a furnace. How I wish it could always be like this. I twist around in his arms, turning to face him.

As always, he reads my thoughts and places a finger to my lips. "Don't," he whispers and turns away, but not before I see the raw emotion crease his face, the moisture in his eyes. I pull him back against me and he squeezes my arm. This is how we have to be, you see; each strong for the other. We couldn't cope, otherwise.

Slowly I rise, reluctant to leave the warmth of his body and the contentment that his closeness brings, but my stomach growls and I realise I'm starving, having skipped lunch to squeeze in a visit to the hairdresser followed by a dash around the deli. It was important to ensure everything was prepared for our evening so that we don't waste a moment of our precious time together.

Carefully, I place the dishes of lobster, potato salad and crusty bread on the table. He looks at them in surprise, then raises an inquisitive eyebrow.

"I know, I know – I just want everything to be perfect."

He reaches over, takes my hand and slowly raises it to his lips. His eyes darken to chocolate and desire springs between us, so tangible we could reach out and touch it. Deliberately he picks up his glass.

"I propose a toast to us and our rainbow Fridays. May there always be sunshine after the rain."

I blink back the tears, which are always never far away these days, I'm determined not to ruin these moments together.

"To us and our rainbow Fridays," I whisper and we clink glasses, aware as always that the toast is bittersweet, the future uncertain.

Realising the mood threatens to turn sombre, he smiles and tucks into the food with relish while I attempt to force delicate morsels past the lump that has lodged in my throat. I ask him about his day. He doesn't ask about mine. That's not part of the game. We don't look to the future or make any plans. We can't. Instead we live in the moment, grateful for the opportunity to be together.

I feel so feminine and desirable

Finally, he grunts in appreciation and pushes away his empty plate. "Best meal I've had for a month," he declares and I nod because I know that it's true. It's not just the food; it's being able to chat and catch up without any interruption.

He rises from the table, turns up the volume on the music and holds out his arms. "I believe they're playing our tune. Shall we dance?"

Together we move around the tiny space between the table and sofa. We don't need much room as we hold each other tightly, swaying, lost in our thoughts and memories, warm in our love. The music changes again; Love is all around us, filling the room.

"Remember when…" he starts, but this time I press my finger to his lips. How could I not remember the most important day of my life? I close my eyes and vividly see us leading the first dance at our reception. Could it really be only two incredibly short years ago?

He stops, sighs and looks deep into my eyes. "It seems a lifetime ago." His voice cracks and I nearly lose it. Fiercely I pull him against me and, as we comfort each other, myriad emotions tumble around in our minds. Sadness, disbelief, bitterness, acceptance, warmth from the comfort of the other, love, desire, until finally our bodies cry out for release from the tension and frustrations that have built steadily over the past month.

"I love you, Kristy," he murmurs and my heart sings. We have survived another month fraught with the worries, responsibilities and sheer physical exhaustion of living with a son with profound special needs. Our darling Toby, born with a perfect body, but with a mind that will forever remain locked in that of a baby. We call him our Peter Pan, for he'll never grow up and we have been warned he might not be with us for long. We don't know.

All we can do now is love him and provide him with the best care we possibly can, but it's hard going, for his needs are always constant.

"I love you, Kristy," he murmurs and my heart soars. I know we'll make it

It was my wonderful mother-in-law who suggested we return to my studio flat each month and spend a few precious hours together as a married couple while she looks after Toby. I gaze at my husband, secure in our love, content to have this time together to gather strength for the road ahead, which the doctors have warned will be rough.

It's ironic, really. Before we married, we travelled the world together, yet none of the challenges we faced could have prepared us for this, the toughest journey of all. But it's a journey we're making together – step-by-step and side by side.

FROM THE AUTHOR

"I have an avid interest in people and colours. A chance remark, stormy weekend and spectacular rainbow sparked this story."

Fancy That!

Fascinating facts that make you go "wow"!

Oldest Oak

The Marton Oak in Cheshire, England, is thought to be 1200 years old

WOW! ● Circus performers consider it unlucky to wear green in the ring.

● **Parakeets have bred in the wild in Britain since the 1960s.**

● In heraldic symbolism, green (known by its heraldic name "vert") represents hope, joy and loyalty in love.

● **The difference between grasses and sedges is that sedges have three-sided stems while grass stems are, in fact, tubular.**

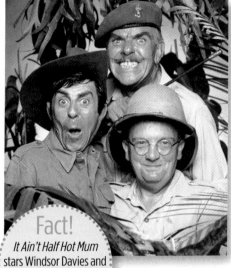

Fact!

It Ain't Half Hot Mum stars Windsor Davies and Don Estelle topped the charts with *Whispering Grass* in 1975

● According to wedding lore, if you marry in green, you're ashamed to be seen.

WOW! ● **Emerald is the birthstone of people born in May.**

● The emerald wedding anniversary is the 55th.

The First Cut Is The Deepest

The first recorded sale of a lawnmower was to a Mr Curtis, head gardener of Regent's Park Zoo, in 1831

WORDS: DOUGLAS MCPHERSON
PICTURES: ALAMY, BBC,
ISTOCKPHOTO, JUPITER IMAGES

The Place

Sit back, relax and enjoy this story of a lucky find that is set to become a favourite piece of furniture

By Glyn Gregg

This looks a good place to start. Sure to have a few Roman coins here."

Very reluctantly, Delia Wilson followed her husband Bill into the dim interior of an antique shop down a back street in Carlisle. She'd spent all weekend following him along Hadrian's Wall and around several extremely informative, yet boring, museums, and she was now completely Roman-soldiered out.

She knew Bill wanted to add to his collection, but all Delia wanted was a cup of tea and a chance to

down and see what developed.

Bill made his way to the little glassed-in office and Delia wandered to the back of the shop, looking idly at a collection of Victorian cake plates and mismatched silverware while she waited for him.

The table on which they were displayed was far more interesting. Old oak, once scrubbed but now badly stained, with a big crack running down the centre. The edges were stippled and indented with age and the chunky turned legs had been painted long ago in an unattractive dark brown.

Delia ran her hand gently across

The first line of a new poem had been skipping in and out of her head all day

take off her shoes. Old junk usually left her unmoved; besides, she'd always felt one antique buff in the family was enough. The first line of a poem had been skipping in and out of her head all day and she couldn't wait to go home, write it

the surface. It was warm and silky to the touch and she felt an odd familiarity. Then she saw the initials carved on one edge – and she knew she had to have this table. Just had to.

"Don't be silly," said Bill,

For A Poet

A lakeland refuge

DOVE COTTAGE

ILLUSTRATIONS: DAVID MATYSIAK

irritable that his coin quest had been unsuccessful. "It's filthy. And anyway, I thought you wanted a small table for your writing. Not this enormous thing."

"I've changed my mind. Oh Bill, don't you see the initials? DW and WW. That's us! We're meant to have this table!"

"Now you're being ridiculous."

The dealer appeared, beaming.

"Lovely old piece, isn't it? Came from a farmhouse near here. It's a real working table, this is; been in the family kitchen there for well over a hundred years. The table itself is at least two hundred, I'd

than two hundred years old!"

"Mmm," Bill grunted, unimpressed by a mere two centuries. He collected valuable Roman and Greek coins as investments, and preferred his silver denarii or gold staters to be in good condition with some sort of provenance.

"You realise it's big enough to seat at least ten people?"

"So? All the better for dinner parties," she retorted airily.

Delia was unable to stop herself smiling. The table obviously had such potential. She could feel the karma and the good vibrations

The table had such potential, she could feel the good vibrations as she polished

say. They really made things to last in those days, didn't they?"

"Two hundred years? It's a piece of history," she whispered, ecstatic. "Bill, we have to buy this."

In the end, they drove home with the table firmly strapped to the top of the car, her husband's face set in grim disapproval.

"I'll clean it up," Delia promised. "I'll scrub it and sand it down a bit. Strip the paint off the legs. And I'll rub it with beeswax and linseed oil, like antique dealers do. It'll look wonderful, I promise. Imagine – it's more

filtering down through the roof of the car. She was sure she'd write the most wonderful poems and stories sitting at it. Ones that would be published.

Cleaning it up took a lot longer than she'd anticipated, but the result was as beautiful as she'd hoped. The old oak glowed with a golden sheen and the table sat solidly in the middle of the dining room, looking as though it had been settled there for years. The initials DW and WW were deeply incised but once she'd

The old gold oak glowed

crossing out, re-writing, or going for walks to encourage her muse.

Three verses were finished within half an hour. Three good verses, she knew, although she would show this to her writer's circle before submitting it to *Poetry Monthly.*

Delia had a very good feeling about this poem.

She made herself a cup of tea and rewarded herself with a chocolate biscuit, sipping while she re-read her work. Idly, her finger traced the letters on the table. DW. Delia Wilson. WW. William Wilson.

rubbed up the timber she found another, more delicate, signature, MW, carved lightly into the surface next to them.

She tried to picture MW as a girl; a younger sister, perhaps. Shyer, more tentative than her stubbornly determined brothers D and WW who'd ensured they'd made their mark in no uncertain terms.

The autumn poem that had been skittering around in her head all week demanded to be put on to paper. She placed her writing folder on the table, unscrewed her fountain pen and began.

*All the leaves are turned to gold
And fallen to the cold black sod.
The branches stark and twisted*

The words flowed out almost faster than she could write them down. Usually she sat for hours,

MW? If she and Bill had ever had children, she would have liked to call their son Michael. Maybe Michael William Wilson. But there had been no children, and the room she'd always thought would be the nursery was now fitted with shelves around each wall and housed Bill's collection of trays of rare coins, catalogued and kept under lock and key.

She began to wonder about the children who had carved these. Had they been sitting doing homework and rebelliously cut the letters under cover of their books? Surely no mother would allow them to do this openly. Had they been farmer's sons? The table had come from near Carlisle.

Then she had a sudden moment of clarity, a fireball that came from out of nowhere.

Grasmere. Dorothy Wordsworth. William Wordsworth and Mary Wordsworth. It had to be!

William and his sister Dorothy had lived at Dove Cottage in Grasmere, and been joined by Mary when William married. What date had that been?

With shaking hands, Delia found her *Lives of British Poets* and paged through. The Wordsworths had occupied Dove Cottage at Grasmere from 1799 to 1808, then they'd moved to Allan Bank, a bigger house in the same town.

She sat down, feeling weak at the knees. This table must be the very one that William Wordsworth had used when he worked.

No wonder my poem just about wrote itself, she thought, elated. *Wait until Bill hears this!*

That evening she rushed out to meet his car and almost dragged him inside, just bubbling with excitement about her discovery.

"You're daft, woman," muttered Bill, but she could tell he was intrigued. He walked around the table, frowning. "So this MW was Wordsworth's wife, then?"

"Yes, Mary Hutchinson. They were friends from their childhood years, they all knew each other," Delia said impatiently. "Don't you see? It's got to be them."

"Well, if you're right, this is even better than a first edition of one of Wordsworth's books! It could well

be worth a whole lot of money."

"Well, yes, but we don't want to sell it," protested Delia, alarmed. "It's just so wonderful to think that we have it."

"I'll find someone who might be able to verify this," Bill said, ignoring her. "That fellow I met from the National Trust might be able to help."

"I won't part with it," Delia said stubbornly. "I don't care if he says it's what we think it is. But leave it Bill – I was just being silly. It probably isn't Wordsworth at all."

It was no use. She heard Bill making some phone calls and the following afternoon, an elderly man knocked on the door and offered his card. *Gerald Macleod, Evaluations and Appraisals of Antique Furniture*, she read.

"Mr Wilson asked me to call," he said. "I believe you have recently acquired an oak table that you

The words flew from the pen

think might be of some historical and literary significance?"

"Yes, but I don't want to sell it," she said immediately. "And I'm sure I'm wrong about the literary significance part. So there's really no point –"

"Just a look," said Mr Macleod mildly. "Simply to advise you on

the charm of these older family pieces, I find." He glanced at her and added diffidently, "I have two poems in the latest issue of *Poet's Monthly*, actually."

"Oh, congratulations! You must be thrilled. I subscribe to that. I'll look out for them."

"I see what you mean about this

"I see what you mean about this table, there's… something about it…"

the saleability at some future date. Or not, of course…"

Delia led him through to the dining room. He looked intently at the table and ran his hands along the surface. She could tell he was appreciating the fine oak grain.

"I've already found it's such an inspiration to sit and write poetry here," she said quietly. "This table has something special about it."

"You write poetry? So do I," Gerald Macleod said, beaming. "Ever been published?"

"Only in the church magazine. And I was runner-up in the *Chronicle* Christmas poem competition, though they didn't print it. But I think the poem I wrote yesterday, sitting at this table, is the best thing I've ever done. So I live in hope."

"Ah, don't we all." He sat down and ran his hand along the grain "Beautiful wood," he commented. "The distress marks always add to

table. There's… something about it." He stood up again and walked slowly around it.

When he came to the initials he studied them for what seemed like a very long time.

"You were lucky to find this," he murmured, almost to himself. He got down on his haunches, patted the legs and peered under the surface of the table top. Then he rose and dusted his hands.

He's going to tell me it's worth a fortune and I'm going to have the most ghastly row with Bill, Delia thought miserably. *But I will not sell this table.*

"I'm sorry, Mrs Wilson, but I don't think this piece is any older than one hundred and twenty years at the most. And William Wordsworth died in 1850, so if you do the sums…"

"But it's typical country-style furniture of the period, well made and sturdy, of course, and I'm sure it will last you a lifetime."

"Oh! Thank you." Delia wasn't sure whether to be devastated or delighted.

"So my husband won't want to sell it, then?"

"I shouldn't think so. I'll send him a written report this afternoon. But it's really a very good work table, isn't it? As one poet to another, I think you've found yourself an exceptionally suitable place on which to compose some special work."

Inspirational!

The valuation expert seemed sure that there could be no literary connection

What a nice man, thought Delia as she closed the door. *He'd sounded quite envious. But the initials – I was so sure. Well, I guess he's the expert and if Wordsworth died before this table was made, I can't argue with that.*

Disconsolate, she went through to the kitchen and put on the kettle.

Later that day, the phone rang.

"Mrs Wilson? Gerald Macleod. I've written a report for your husband, as he asked. But I just wanted to stress – as one poet to another – that experts aren't infallible, you know. They've been known to make mistakes."

"Oh."

What was he telling her?

"If you look very carefully under the table directly below the incised initials, you'll find the outline of a bird. I don't think you noticed this before, did you? Have a good look and see if you can identify it."

Somehow Delia knew exactly what she was going to find on the underside of the table.

The outline of a perfect little dove. Scratched one evening by one of the sentimental Wordsworths, perhaps just before they moved from Dove Cottage…

FROM THE AUTHOR

"I love old furniture and trawling through antique shops. The idea of finding something belonging to a writer just felt right!"

Fancy That!

Fascinating facts that make you go "wow"!

Mind The Gap

The pink route on the London Underground map is the Hammersmith Line, which opened in 1864

Fact!
Cadillacs are named after the French explorer who founded Detroit, where the cars are made

WOW! ● *Lily The Pink* was the only Number One hit for the Scaffold, in 1968.
● **The *Financial Times* was first published on February 13, 1888.**

● The first ballet was *Le Ballet Comique de La Reine*, and was performed in 1581 for Catherine de Medici, Queen of France.

● **According to superstition, if you marry in pink, your spirits will sink.**

WOW! ● Britain is France's biggest customer for champagne.
● **The skin on our fingers and palms has more sweat glands than other parts of the body, to help improve our grip.**

In The Pink

In the John Travolta and Olivia Newton-John film *Grease*, the boys are the T-Birds and the girls are the Pink Ladies

WORDS: DOUGLAS MCPHERSON
PICTURES: ALAMY, ALLSTAR PICTURE LIBRARY, ISTOCKPHOTO

Face The Music!

Ever wished you could leave all the family rows behind and disappear to the Med?

By Olivia Davis

Alan Morrison waited for a gap in the traffic that streamed westward to Gibraltar along the coastal road. When his chance came, he accelerated the elderly, but bravely crimson, Mercedes convertible out of the driveway that curved downhill from El Tropicana urbanisation.

"Do you have to do that quite so dramatically?" Della demanded as the slipstream tousled her sun-bleached hair.

Alan grinned. "I'm not driving in suburbia now," he said and gave a blast on the car's air-tone horn as a salutation to the hippy girl waiting by the bus stop.

Della laughed. "And you're not dressed for suburbia," she said. "That fruit-salad shirt. And your cut-off jeans! They'll be horrified. You might have soft-pedalled for our first meeting after so long. And they'll moan about the length of your hair."

"And what about you? It might have been an idea to wear something to hide that tattoo. Give them a chance to get used to how we are, kind of gradual-like."

"They'll have to accept it or lump it. I always craved a rose tattoo on my arm, but I didn't dare in England. You can imagine the upset it would have caused. But now I've got one."

She caressed the colourful example of the tattooist's art and for a while neither spoke. To their left, the sun turned the Mediterranean into a dazzling mirror on which could be seen, if you were wearing sunglasses, a line of boats returning to Estepona after a night's fishing.

"How I love it here,"
Della breathed

Gazing out, Della exclaimed, "Oh, how I love this place!"

Alan glanced at her. "You've no regrets, then?"

"No, Well, perhaps a few. Sometimes I do wonder whether we did the right thing. I mean, running away in the night and leaving them like that."

"It was the only way. If we'd tried to talk it over, they'd never have understood – it would have been a blazing argument for weeks. And I was up to my neck in arguments. I was sick of their criticism, sick of them sneering at our music, sick of their superior attitude – that look they gave each other when I tried to put any of my ideas forward."

"Yes, that got me – that eyes-up-to-heaven look. Still, I suppose that's the generation gap for you. There must be thousands and

Sick of all the disapproval, they'd left a note on the table, packed up and gone

thousands of homes like ours was."

"Yes, but we had the bottle to quit – to do our own thing."

"If it hadn't been for Aunt Cindy leaving us that money, we couldn't have done it – unless we'd moved into cardboard boxes."

"There were times when I thought that would've been better. Remember when they arrived home early and we were having that party? Those remarks about the way we were dancing!"

"I didn't dare see my friends for ages after that. What they must have thought!"

"They probably understood. Wayne and Marlene were having the same problem. When he forgot and lit a cigarette in front of them...! God bless Aunt Cindy is all I can say. We must have been her favourites."

"God bless Aunt Cindy. But sometimes I wonder… well, was it right to leave them just like that? I've often wondered how they coped, alone in the house." Della frowned thoughtfully.

"Pretty well, I should think. It didn't have a mortgage, they both have jobs and they obviously knew more about life than us – or so they think. They'd be perfectly okay without us to worry about." He laughed. "I'd love to have been a fly on the wall when they came down to breakfast and saw the note on the table."

Della giggled. "*We've had*

enough. So long and goodbye!"

"Perhaps it was a bit dramatic, but I could see no other way. Imagine what it'd have been like if we'd broken it to them gently that we were clearing out to the Costa del Sol. The lectures, the talk of irresponsibility, how we owed it to them to stay. Anyway, they've deigned to come and see us."

"You know, Alan, I must admit, I'm nervous about this meeting. I mean, they always have some sort of hold over you, no matter how you've chosen to rebel."

"Just remember, we're grown up. We have as much right to our way of life as they have to theirs. If they can now accept that, it may be all right. They weren't bad, just impossible. As you said, the generation gap… In the old days I guess one generation was pretty much like the previous one, but now everything can

They headed for the airport

change so quickly. Take music."

"No, thank you. One of the joys of being out here is playing my CDs without seeing those expressions of horror."

They turned off the highway and followed the road to La Linea, beyond which reared the Rock of

tactful thing is to try and be nice."

"Nice! After all the anxiety they gave us! But I suppose you're right. I shall be controlled."

"Here goes," said William as they left Customs.

Ahead was the usual crowd of eager friends, relatives and car hire

"I don't believe it," William muttered, seeing the couple waiting for them…

Gibraltar. Soon they crossed the frontier and, minutes later were waiting at the arrivals gate at the Gibraltar Airport where the Monarch aircraft from Luton was rolling to a stop on the runway.

William and Sarah Morrison glanced at each other as they piloted a baggage trolley through the Nothing To Declare area.

"It's stupid, but I feel nervous," murmured Sarah. "I mean, they are our own flesh and blood – but what does one say to them? Do we pretend they didn't run away from home without a thought for us, a year ago, and say, 'Hello, you two, you're looking well'? That is, if they *are* looking well. I hate to think of the sort of life they've been leading down here."

"They'll have probably changed a bit," mused William. Although he was wearing a summerweight jacket, his face was already sheened with perspiration. "The

representatives holding up large placards with customers' names printed or scrawled on them.

"I don't believe it!" muttered William. In the centre of the group was a figure in shorts and a vivid Hawaiian shirt. He was tanned, had hair down to his shoulders and sported a chunky gold bracelet. Beside him was a bronzed woman wearing a tight cerise T-shirt emblazoned "Crazy Rocker". Had it been an advertisement for a bordello, it could not have jarred Sarah more.

William gulped in a deep breath and then strode forward manfully.

"Hi, Mum," he said. "Hi, Dad."

FROM THE AUTHOR

"On the Costa Del Sol I saw a couple in their middle years wearing teenage fashions. That was enough to trigger my imagination."

Jamie's Gift

Your heart will be touched by this tale of the bond of understanding that can bridge the generations

By Sheila Ireland

From the rear seat of the car came Jamie's voice. "What's it like being blind, Mum?" The seven-year-old had his eyes tight shut and could feel his head starting to spin. It was weird.

"Is it like this?" He stretched his hands out and began fumbling around the tops of the front seats.

"Jamie, open your eyes this minute. And please stop that!" Mary Ackroyd swung round in the passenger's seat and glared at her son. *Children can be so insensitive,* she thought, turning towards her husband in dismay. "Jack, I'm so very worried…"

"I know, love." Taking his hand from the steering wheel, he briefly touched her arm gently. "But everything's going to be all right."

He glanced round at his son. "Just stop your nonsense right this very minute, please, Jamie."

Jamie opened his eyes and sighed. He was always doing something wrong. His nose was itchy, so he rubbed it hard with the back of his hand. He looked out of the car window.

"Hey – cows!" he yelled, and pressed his nose against the glass.

Mary sat back in her seat. They'd been travelling for quite a few hours now but, thankfully, they'd soon be driving on the country road that led to her parents' retirement cottage.

She wondered if the weather was as hot at home in London as it was here in Yorkshire. The heat

It seems this lively lad can do nothing right. But he might just help his gran

had withered the grass at the sides of the dusty road and a shimmering summer haze hung over the hills ahead.

I have no idea what it must be like to be blind, she thought. It was something she didn't want to even think about – yet the question had

At last he could help

haunted her, ever since the phone call from her dad a week ago.

It wasn't a long call. Her father had never been one for chatting over the phone. He usually just said what had to be said. But this time his voice was sad, and he took longer to get the words out.

"Your mum's gone blind, Mary," he'd said. It had happened just as the doctors had predicted, sudden and irreversible, despite all these years of careful observation and then treatment.

"She woke up this morning and didn't know what to do, love. I'm not sure how she'll cope."

Mary blinked back a tear. Her mother was Yorkshire born and bred and wouldn't take kindly to anyone's pity, nor accept advice easily. She'd always been fiercely proud and independent. It would be hard for her to come to terms with what had happened.

Mary sighed and looked at the road ahead. In the rear of the car, her son was beginning to get more than a little boisterous again.

Jamie was restless. They were driving along a little road now; no cows or sheep, just grass and some old trees. Boring. He swung his legs and drummed his heels on the panel underneath his seat.

His father impatiently said, "Stop that, Jamie."

Jamie pulled a face and sat still. He was fed up now. He wished they'd hurry up and get to Gran's house. He always had a good time on his holidays with his gran. She took him for walks and played with him and made him laugh.

This time it would be just as good, maybe even better. He slumped down in his seat. He knew his gran was blind now, and that everyone was sad about it. But he'd never met anyone who was

blind, and he was curious and even a bit excited.

Anyway, she was nice, his gran. She used to be a teacher and was always showing him stuff, like how to ride his bike and make paper aeroplanes. She'd even shown him how to read before he went to school. Jamie smiled. Sometimes that had been hard; he'd got stuck and wanted to give up. But his gran wouldn't let him.

"Sometimes you have to grit your teeth to make your brain work better, Jamie." She did it herself, then, to show him, pulling a face that was very funny and making him laugh.

"Never give up, Jamie." She'd ruffled his hair. "It's

He always had fun at Gran's

doing the tough things that make you clever and strong and brave. Be brave, lad. Just try. Do it for me. Please, love."

Jamie was glad he had carried on. After a while, he had got over the hard stuff and now he could read his comic books himself. It was fun, now. He sighed impatiently. He was looking forward to seeing his gran, he just wished they would hurry up and get there soon.

Mary and her husband, Jack, exchanged glances as they pulled up outside her parents' cottage,

lass. She's a stubborn woman, your mother. Doesn't want anyone's help, yet can't really help herself. She just sits around, saying nothing. Ignores me when I try to talk to her. I think she's in shock. It's a bad do."

"And Social Services?"

"Your mum told the lady to go away; she didn't want her help." Her father sounded tired. "I've been trying all week to get your mum to use the white stick they gave her; it would help her get about a bit. But she's having none of it. It's hard to know what to do

"Jamie?" she said uncertainly, raising her head as he clattered towards her

and could see only her father was standing, waiting to greet them.

"Your mum's sitting out in the back garden, Mary," her dad explained as they all emerged from the car.

Jamie bolted from the back seat, jumped into his granddad's arms for a hug, and then tore off down the garden path, shrieking, "Gran! We're here!"

"Jamie!" Mary called after him worriedly. "Don't you go bothering your grandma!" She might just as well have tried to stop a runaway train.

Sighing, she turned to her father. "How is she, Dad?"

He shook his head. "Not good,

for the best." He looked helpless. "Anyway, let's get all your luggage inside, so that you can have a chat with your mum."

Mary left the men to unload the cases from the car and headed for the back garden. She needed to know what Jamie was up to.

Hello, Gran!" Jamie yelled happily, running across the lawn. His grandmother was sitting on a garden chair at a table with a bright red-and-white striped sun umbrella. She wore a floppy straw hat, floral dress and white pumps.

"Jamie?" she said uncertainly, and raised her head. Her face was lined and deeply tanned by the sun, so that her greying hair seemed white and her pale blue eyes alive and startlingly clear. She stretched out her hand. "Jamie…"

"I'm here, Gran," Jamie said, taking her hand and letting himself be hugged and kissed, which he didn't like much. He pulled away and looked at his grandmother. He was disappointed. He'd thought she might be wearing dark glasses or that her eyes would be closed or something. Puzzled, he blurted out, "Gran, you don't really look like you're blind."

His grandmother stiffened and blinked and her jaw tightened.

"What's it like, Gran?" Jamie

green stems and big leaves where the caterpillars and ladybirds crawled, while bees and insects buzzed and droned. Jamie wondered what all this was like for his grandmother.

"The lady next door told Mum that blind people can hear better than other people," he said. "Can you hear better now, Gran?"

His grandmother didn't answer. Her lips went a bit thin, that was all. Jamie frowned and tried again.

"At school, when something's really hard, I shut my eyes so I can think better. Can you think better than other people now, Gran?"

Again, his grandmother didn't

"I'm really worried, Dad. It's as if she's lost interest in – well, everything"

moved closer so that his knees touched his grandmother's, and he reached up inquisitively to touch her face gently with his fingers.

"Jamie – no! Don't do that!" She pulled her face away from his hand, and for a moment she looked very fierce. Jamie leapt back, alarmed.

Then his grandmother relented. "Sorry, lad," she said softly, "but you shouldn't touch your gran's face sudden like that."

"Sorry, Gran." Jamie slipped his hand into hers. The garden looked nice with the sun shining. The busy flowerbeds were full of white and red and golden flowers with bright

answer, and Jamie wasn't sure what was happening. It was then that he saw his mother hurrying towards them.

"Jamie, I told you not to go bothering your gran right now!" she cautioned.

Jamie looked down at his shoes, knowing he was in trouble again. But when he looked up, his mother had her arms around his gran and there were tears in her eyes. So he slipped away and went to play by the big tree in the garden.

Later that evening, when

He'd heard everything…

Jamie and his grandmother had gone to bed, Mary, Jack, and her father sat outside on the veranda and spoke in private and anguished tones. "She's not accepting her blindness, not facing up to it at all," Mary lamented. "It's as if she's lost interest in… everything. Dad, I'm really worried about her."

Her father nodded.

"It can't be easy," Jack put in quietly. "Maybe it's best to let her be – just let her have some time to adjust to what's happened."

"We should give her our comfort and support, but not make any demands on her," Mary agreed. "I'll try to make sure Jamie doesn't go bothering her." She sighed. "I think she's just given up."

The night sky was a deep starlit blue and the three of them sat for a while in its glow. But there were no more answers, and soon they got up and went to bed.

Upstairs in his bedroom with its window open, Jamie was still awake. He had overheard his parents' conversation, and their words echoed in his mind now and wouldn't go away. He pushed his head deep down into his pillow. Eventually he fell asleep.

The next morning, Jamie woke up to the sound of a church bell ringing from some distance off. If he'd been at home, he would be going to Sunday school, he remembered. There, they all sat in a big circle and listened to stories from the Bible. Some really good stories, too. He got up and went to clean his teeth, still thinking about that and smiling to himself.

Later, he was playing on his own when he found his grandmother's white stick on a chair. He took it outside with him so that he could play Zorro and twirl it like a sword above his head.

The sun was hot and bright and he was enjoying himself, swiping wildly at the enemy, when his grandmother was brought outside.

"Jamie!" his mother called out. "Put that stick down, please."

He stopped in mid-swipe and his heart fell. He didn't think he'd been doing anything wrong.

His mother came and took the walking stick out of his hand. Jamie bowed his head and kicked at the grass with his toes. His grandmother was sitting under the umbrella again, her back stiff against the back of her seat. He wondered if she would ever take him a walk in the forest again. It wasn't far, only just down the road, and they could hold hands. Maybe a blind person could do that.

Jamie remembered something, then, and he sidled over and got close to her. He stood on his tiptoes and whispered, "Samson was blind, too, Gran…"

His grandmother blinked and her mouth opened in surprise, but she said nothing.

Jamie sighed, a little exasperated. He wanted her to talk to him, like she used to. He remembered something else.

"Blind people have dogs, Gran," he whispered excitedly. "Labradors. Are you going to get a Labrador? That would be great, Gran, wouldn't it?"

And he thought his gran might have smiled then but he wasn't sure, for the adults came to sit around the table and started asking how she was. He went and found his

ball and played with it on the lawn.

Later, Jamie sat under the tree, just watching. All the adults were sitting in chairs around the table, talking to his grandmother. Only nobody was laughing like they used to on holiday and Jamie thought they were probably giving her comfort and support, like they'd said. But it didn't seem like much to him.

He sat and waited. His chance came when he saw his mum and dad and granddad get up and go inside, probably to make a pot of tea and sandwiches for lunch. His grandmother was on her own and Jamie went quietly across to

How could he help?

her. He was going to tell her that blind people could do amazing things, even read with their fingers. But he stopped short, because his gran was sitting there, quietly talking to herself.

"Nobody understands," she was saying. "They've never been blind, yet they all think they can tell you what to do. But they don't know, none o' them." She shook her head. "Daft, if you ask me," she muttered under her breath.

Jamie didn't know what to say. He desperately wanted to help, but didn't know how.

"Hello, Gran," he whispered.

His grandmother stiffened in her chair. "Jamie, is that you?"

Jamie went up and gently took

"You just won't ever give up, will you, lad?"

Jamie grinned. Suddenly he knew just what to say.

"You taught me not to, Gran," he said. "You told me to grit my teeth, remember?" He looked at her closely. "You haven't given up, have you, Gran?"

His grandmother frowned. "It's not so easy for me, Jamie."

Jamie remembered himself saying just that once.

"It's doing the tough things that make you strong and brave," he recited from memory.

His grandmother became very still. There was no sound in the garden. It was warm and pleasant in the sunshine. Jamie waited.

"What is it that you want of me,

Jamie remembered what she'd told him. "Be brave. Just try. Do it for me"

her hand. "Blind people can read with their fingers, Gran," he said.

His grandmother sighed softly. "Oh, please, stop it, Jamie."

He was very close to her now and he saw the tears in her eyes. He frowned. He'd never seen his gran cry before.

He squeezed her hand gently. "I'm sorry, Gran."

She smiled then, a little shakily, maybe, but it was a smile and it gave Jamie some hope.

lad?" his gran asked wearily.

"I want us to go for a walk, just like we used to."

His gran closed her eyes and moaned softly. "I'm blind, Jamie. I don't know if I can do that."

Jamie remembered. "Be brave, Gran. Just try. Try to do it for me. Please just try."

At that, his grandmother reached out and pulled him into her arms. She hugged him close for a long time. So Jamie didn't see her tighten her jaw and grit her teeth.

Jamie managed to get into the house without anyone seeing him. He found his grandmother's walking stick propped up against the small phone table in the hall, and he grabbed it and ran. But he only got as far as the edge of the lawn.

Together they found the answer

"Let the boy be, Mary. I asked him to bring the stick. We're off for a walk"

"Jamie!" his mother called after him. "Come back here, please."

He skidded to a stop hearing her voice, his heart plummeting.

"Oh, Jamie." His mother came towards him, looking weary. "Give me the stick, please."

Jamie stood there in the hot sun, unsure what to do. Finally he said, "Gran asked me for it, Mum. She told me to fetch it for her."

His mother looked at him, puzzled by what was going on.

"Let the boy be, Mary!" his grandmother called out from across the garden. "I asked him to bring me the stick. We're going for a walk, and I'm goin' to need it for a while, at least till I'm used to things."

Mary opened her mouth but

nothing came out. She looked down at her son. "What on earth did you do, Jamie?" she asked softly, in amazement.

Jamie shrugged. He wasn't sure. He just knew that, this time, for the first time, it must have been something right at last.

He ran towards his grandmother, waving her stick aloft like a sword. "I'm coming, Gran," he shouted.

FROM THE AUTHOR

"This story could well be called *Through The Eyes Of A Child*, but this particular child is a very special boy, I'm sure you agree."

Teatime Treats

Triple Layer Bounty Bars

CHOC & COCONUT

Ingredients

- 350g (12oz) quality milk chocolate
- 100g (4oz) quality dark chocolate
- 100g (4oz) butter, softened
- 100g (4oz) icing sugar, sifted
- 200g (7oz) condensed milk (half regular can)
- 225g (8oz) dessiccated coconut

Preparation time: 20mins + 2hrs chilling

Makes: 30

- Line a 23x33cm (9x13inch) swiss roll tin with greaseproof paper.
- Melt 300g (10½oz) of the **milk chocolate** and 50g (2oz) of the **dark chocolate** in a microwave or in a bowl over a pan of simmering water until melted. Stir, then spread evenly over base of the tin. Set aside to let it harden.
- Mix **butter** and **sugar** together, then stir in **condensed milk** and **coconut**. Spread this mixture evenly over the chocolate layer and level out with a palette knife.
- Melt remaining milk and dark chocolate together as before, then drizzle over the coconut layer. Set aside to harden, then cut into 30 bars.

RECIPE: SUE LAWRENCE STYLING: MAXINE CLARK
PHOTOGRAPHY: LIGHTHOUSE PHOTOGRAPHY

Simmer Gently

Who would think that a jar of pickle could bring a flavour of romance to my life?

By Linda Lewis

The whole thing would never have happened, had I not offered Paula some home-made strawberry jam.

"You know, this is really good." I watched her slap another spoonful of jam on to a slice of bread. "You could sell this," she said between mouthfuls. "Make a fortune."

"I wouldn't know where to start," I demurred. "Besides, I do it for therapy, not for profit."

Paula licked her fingers extravagantly and I laughed. "Take with jars of pickles. "I can't seem to stop myself."

Paula smiled indulgently. She knew why I kept busy making jam and pickles. It made up for what was missing from my life – romance. Sometimes I wondered how I managed to have such great friends. They've seen so much more of life than I have.

Then Paula asked the question that would change my life. "Can I take some jars to work? I'm raising money for the British Heart Foundation," she explained. "This stuff will fly. It's delicious."

"Take as much as you like. Just

Little did I know that offering Paula some jam was going to change my life

some home. I've got lots more."

I opened a cupboard door and Paula gasped. "Good grief!" she said. "There must be thirty pots of jam in there."

"Thirty-four," I admitted. I opened another cupboard, stacked

ask people to return the jars when they're finished."

Paula giggled. "Good old Megan. Always careful."

I didn't mind her teasing. I was careful with money; I'd had to be.

Mum had always been frail.

Making jam was my therapy

Soon after Dad died in a car accident, it became clear she needed full-time help. I moved in with her, losing both my job and my boyfriend in the process.

It wasn't much of a sacrifice. Mum and I had always been close,

and my relationship with Patrick wasn't going anywhere.

I soon got used to being careful with money. Then Mum had a series of small strokes. It got to the point where I couldn't take care of her any longer. Last summer, she went to live in a lovely nursing home, and I went back to work in a hotel kitchen. Money was no longer a problem, but I couldn't break the being-careful habit. I was recycling before the term was even invented.

Paula left, balancing two boxes of jam and pickles. I went straight out into the garden, to harvest some beans, cauliflower, and onions, then set about making more pickle.

Paula popped round the following evening. "I sold some piccalilli to my boss. He said it reminded him of the pickles his Gran made. He wants to meet you!"

"Whatever for?"

"I don't know. Maybe he wants the recipe. He said, 'Whoever made that piccalilli must be a fascinating person'."

"That's silly. I'm not in the least bit fascinating."

"Yes, you are."

"Now stop that," I said firmly. I'd played that game with Paula too many times. "Who is this pickle-loving person?"

"Our new branch manager, David. He's just moved here from Watford. That's where you used to live, isn't it?"

"Years ago. We moved when I left school."

"So shall I fix up a meet? He's forty-three, divorced, two grown-up children,

and he looks a bit like Terry Wogan. What do you say? Are you interested?"

I sighed. "No, of course not. I've never been on a blind date and I'm not starting now. Anyway, why would I want to meet somebody who loves pickles?"

Paula frowned. "It's not a date. He just wants to meet you."

Then I had an idea. "Give him Tina's number. She's looking for a new man. He just wants someone who knows their way round a kitchen. We both know Tina's a whiz with the microwave."

I tried to put the whole thing out of my mind, but my curiosity had been aroused. Somewhere a bell was ringing, but I couldn't work out why.

A week later, I called Tina to find out if she and David had hit it off. "How did it go?" I asked her.

"Not great. He seemed disappointed when I showed up, especially when I couldn't tell him how the piccalilli was made."

"Are you seeing him again?"

"No. He kept going on about his grandmother's recipes." She sighed. "In the end I had to own up. I mean, I can't remember the last time I cooked anything more complicated than a roast chicken. He was upset when I said you didn't want to meet him. I don't think it was romance he was

It was as if I couldn't stop

"I just wanted to say thank you," he said. "Tasting your wonderful pickle took me right back to my school days."

"Happy, were they?"

"Mostly. I lived with my grandmother. She was a cookery teacher, domestic science or whatever it was they called it. Her strawberry jam sandwiches were absolutely amazing."

Something prickled at the back of my mind. "Don't tell me her name was Mrs Grainger."

He grinned. "Yep. Hadley Secondary Modern."

"I went there! She taught me to love food, and how to cook."

"I know." He sipped his red wine. "I recognised that piccalilli. It was exactly like Gran used to make. That's one of the reasons I wanted to meet you. There's a school

after; he just wanted to try to make a new friend."

That tapped a raw nerve. I was lucky, I made friends easily, but I knew it wasn't that simple for everyone. Suddenly I'd become the

My curiosity was aroused. A bell was ringing, but I couldn't work out why

Wicked Witch Of The East.

I sighed. "All right. Give him my number. If he calls, I'll meet him after work, in that wine bar behind the cinema."

He rang the very next day. I tried to wheedle my way out of it, but he wouldn't take no for an answer.

Three days later, I found myself in the wine bar. David was waiting when I arrived. He bought me a glass of wine and we sat down.

reunion next month. Do you fancy going? Just for the company," he added quickly.

I thanked him and said no. I couldn't face it. The other people at these things had all done so much more with their lives.

"Shame," he said, then he looked at me with a strange searching expression. "You know, you've still got the greenest eyes I've ever seen."

Then I realised who he was.

"You're Doodling David!" I said.

He laughed. "That's me. I had this major crush on you."

"I remember it well! You drew pictures of me in your notebook."

He grinned. "I've still got some of them. I don't know why I kept them, you were so horrible to me. Remember the art cupboard?"

I did. I'd tempted David inside, then ran out and shut the door, locking him in.

He was there all day until a teacher needed more pencils. It was cruel, but at 16, the last

"Just like my gran used to make"

It was then I told David my secret – the secret I'd never told anyone before…

thing I wanted was a 14-year-old boy trailing around after me.

"Sorry about that," I said, but I couldn't help laughing.

Luckily David laughed, too. "I was traumatised for years after that," he joked.

"It's all coming back to me now. You bought all the pickles I made for the school fete. The box was so heavy, you could hardly carry it."

"I didn't want anybody else to have any of it."

Grinning, he took my hand. "The moment I tasted that piccalilli, I knew it was yours. It sounds crazy, but I think I'm still more than a little in love with you."

It was then I told David my secret – the secret I'd never told

anyone, especially not my best friend at school. You see, he was the first boy I ever really liked – but he was 14 and I was 16. Back then, that age difference was a huge and impossible barrier.

Now, it didn't matter. I thanked my lucky stars for all those hours spent making jam and piccalilli. Thanks to them, my first love had come back into my life.

ABOUT THE AUTHOR

"Once upon a time, I grew my own fruit and vegetables. I made so much jam, I had to give it away. That memory inspired this story."

Fancy That!

Fascinating facts that make you go "wow"!

Grassroots!

Tom Jones first heard *The Green, Green Grass Of Home* on the Jerry Lee Lewis album *Country Songs For City Folks*

WOW! ● **Only the legs of the green sandpiper are actually green. The rest of the bird is brown, grey and white.**
● The meadow grasshopper (Chorthippus parallelus) is Britain's only flightless grasshopper, even though it has wings.
● **Britain's only green butterfly, the Green Hairstreak (Callophrys rubi) is** found mainly on the downs and heaths of the south of England.

Fact!
The green woodpecker is sometimes known as the "yaffle" due to the laughing sound of its call

WOW! ● The Duke of Wellington wore leather boots. The rubber wellies named after him appeared only a year before his death.

Jackie Wilson Says...

Soul singer Al Green was kicked out of his family's gospel group for listening to "profane" Jackie Wilson records

Every Precio

Determined to make the most of her study time, could Sissy be missing out on something else?

By Diane Harrison

T ime seemed to stand still as I sat, perched on a box, in the now empty, silent room. It was the start of a new era for me – but it was an emotional day for all of us.

My mum had kept sniffing into a handkerchief and looking as if the end of the world had arrived, instead of her daughter starting a new life at university.

My dad made comments about the boys I'd meet, as if they were all members of a species I'd never encountered before, and how he hoped I'd be, um, *careful.*

I didn't bother to tease him and ask what he meant. That would've been too awful, watching him squirm and try to come up with an answer that didn't include the words "boys" and "sex" in the same sentence. Dad always talked

about *being careful*, then looked at Mum to fill in the rest.

"I can manage to put things away myself," I said finally, taking my case from Mum.

I knew they meant well. They wanted to help, and didn't want to leave. Then suddenly, with a last frantic burst of hugs and kisses, they were gone and I was alone.

A part of me wanted to call them back. The other part, the "look at me, I'm all grown up" part, wanted to sing and dance and celebrate my new freedom.

I did neither. I just sat on the box and slowly pulled the ribbon from a tissue-wrapped parcel. Mum had thrust it into my hands before leaving and Dad had muttered, "This is something to help you manage your time."

I looked at the present they'd left me and smiled. It was Great-grandma's hourglass – a sort of

The boy across the landing was sweet, but not very committed to his work…

us Moment

I was going to make good use of my time

family heirloom that until now we had used as a paperweight at home. They certainly didn't intend me to waste my time here.

"My goodness! You must like your boiled eggs well cooked…"

At the doorway stood one of those alien creatures Dad had been trying to warn me about.

"It's not an egg timer," I said,

turning the hourglass over in its wooden stand to allow the sand to run through from one bulb to the other. "It's an hourglass. I think my parents thought it would help me with my revision. Like, do an hour, then rest and start again."

It sounded slightly silly, saying this to a gangly six-footer with a lopsided grin, untidy brown hair and grey eyes framed with dark lashes. He moved lithely from the doorway to sit on one of the boxes without waiting for an invitation.

"My parents didn't even give me a three-minute timer. They know my attention span couldn't cope with anything that long."

"Well, I'm here to work."

Did I sound as pompous to him as I did to my own ears? I quickly amended my comment. "I mean, I can't mess up this great chance I have to be at this university."

"Hi" and went our own way. His room, across the hall, was the one where everyone went. He invited me occasionally, but I was too focused to be tempted by his lifestyle of drinking and parties – and, perhaps, a little shy.

Nearer the exams, I noticed all noisy activities stopped in the room across the hall and the lights burned bright all night.

"Are you all right?" I asked the next time we met. Mathew had dark shadows under his eyes.

"Yes. I just wish I'd used even a little three-minute egg timer a few times. You're right, I should have worked more," he said. "Not good on the self-discipline thing. Fancy coming out for a drink?"

"Why don't you just come into my room?"

A grin lit up his face, taking the edge off his slightly gaunt features.

Just as I decided to turn the hourglass, he gently reached out to stop me

"Oh, sure!" he agreed, levering himself up from the box. "I'm Mathew... and you?"

"I'm Celia, although everyone I know usually calls me Sissy."

"Well, try to make time for other things, too, Sissy. Don't forget to enjoy yourself."

I saw Mathew many times during the term. We waved and said

"I meant, come into my room to revise. We can share some wine later," I added, to appease him. "Go and get your books."

I pointedly put the hourglass in the middle of the floor and we squatted down on cushions to work. Neither of us said a word as the sand ran through but, when I reached out after the first hour to turn it over, Mathew's hand ever so

I used the hourglass to time my revision

his door and, rather surprisingly, I thought how much I'd miss him if he hadn't managed to get through all of the exams.

But he turned up the following week, having missed several lectures, with the same lop-sided grin on his face.

"Starting as I mean to go on," he said, holding up an egg timer. "Couldn't aspire to your great heights, but it's a start."

He still partied. He even coaxed yours truly to join in. Occasionally we studied together, although when he got fed up he substituted his timer for mine.

In our final year, we were expected to move out and give up our cloistered rooms to the freshmen who were starting their first year.

It seemed natural for Mathew and me to rent a flat together. I expected my parents to object, even though we had separate single rooms, but I think they were relieved that I wasn't doing anything worse than sharing a flat when left to my own devices in the big, bad world.

Mathew brought girls home, but, hey, it didn't matter because we were only flatmates. I had the occasional platonic boyfriend, but I wasn't interested in anyone.

In the Christmas term I went home briefly and did the turkey thing and the pudding thing and pulled the crackers, but I was glad

gently reached out to stop me.

"The deal was, wine after studying." He gently pulled my blonde ponytail. "You're such a dreadful swot, Sissy!"

"I didn't say how long you'd have to wait!" I laughed. But we drank a glass of vino before doing some more revising.

We spent a lot of time together over the next few weeks. I hadn't realised how nice it was to have some company; especially this someone's company.

When I moved back into the halls of residence the next academic year, I looked out for Mathew. There wasn't a light under to be back at the flat. I think I'd outgrown my family's lifestyle and was happier at university.

Mathew was there when I returned, and he said he liked the way I wore my hair loose; said it accentuated my green eyes. We had our own Christmas party. The next morning I woke up beside him.

I felt sick. How could I have got myself into this situation? I did love Mathew; I realised that, just before I lifted my head from the pillow and saw him there. But I didn't want our relationship to be based on a drunken mistake. And I was sorry that the first time had been so forgettable.

Yet it was difficult to erase that night entirely from my mind.

I kept out of his way, and thankfully he kept out of mine. We were polite to each other, but the relationship, such as it had been, reverted back to those early days when we both did our own thing.

I suppose I noticed something was wrong a few months later. There were no parties, no strange girls wandering around in the mornings. With anyone else, I might have thought it was about exams and studying, but with Mathew that didn't enter my mind.

"You okay?" I asked as I tried to pull some folders from beneath him as he lay on the sofa. "Come on, move, Mathew."

He lifted his feet up off the cushions to oblige. But I could see

He said he liked the way I wore my hair

he would be going nowhere today.

"No lectures, tutorials?" I asked.

"I need to talk to you, Sissy," he said quietly.

"Later," I said avoiding the issue.

I rushed out to lectures. I had to study; no matter if Mathew seemed to be able to prepare for his degree by reading comics or watching TV.

The conversation we would have that evening was inevitable. It was obvious: he didn't want to carry on sharing. That night had made us both uncomfortable.

As they say, another time, another place – and, in our

me want to eat, but I thought I'd do it in style rather than gorge on a chocolate bar alone.

Mathew still didn't move until I cleared the rubbish from the coffee table with a sweep of my arm to make way for the tray there. Magazines, empty crisp packets and plastic cups fell higgledy-piggledy in a pile on the floor.

Mathew didn't notice the mess. He sat up like a zombie and picked idly at the plate of food before turning his attention to the wine. He'd had two glasses and started on the third before he looked at me and took a deep breath.

Here it comes, I thought. *Wham, bam, thank you ma'am.*

"I've had some bad news," he said in abject misery.

I wasn't prepared for this. I'd thought only of myself. It was my turn to pour out the wine.

"I've got a disease," he carried on quietly.

I stared. What on earth? The

particular case, another person.

When I eventually returned, Mathew was still on the sofa, as if he'd not made a move all day long.

"I've had a bit of bad news," he said quietly. I wasn't prepared for this at all

"Come on, lazybones!" I said in great annoyance.

I opened a bottle of wine, got two glasses and placed them on a tray with two forks, while I heated spaghetti carbonara in the microwave and threw a salad together. Bad news always made

only diseases I could think of were nasty ones. Like those you had to tell ex-girlfriends about.

"You what...?"

I couldn't find words to express my feelings. I picked up what was left of the spaghetti carbonara, complete with side salad, and threw it at him. All those girls he'd slept with in the past – the consequences were coming home to roost. And I would be paying the price as well.

Then I became frightened.

"Is it HIV?"

Mathew hadn't bothered to wipe the bits of pasta and bacon from his T-shirt and sat there with the thick

"What type of personality will he have?" he said fondly, as he stood his egg timer by my hourglass.

"He could be a she," I reminded him ever so gently.

"No," he said. He placed his hand on my bump. "I can definitely feel him kicking me."

Everything was fine until Mathew caught a minor infection.

My son has an egg timer personality. I know no other baby so fast or so bright

cream sauce dripping off his face.

"No. I had leukaemia as a child. It's come back."

I'd thought Mathew had avoided me because he regretted the change in our relationship. Not because of something like this. With a breaking heart, I kissed the sauce from his lips.

Mathew didn't get to return to university; his treatments took up too much time and energy. But he wouldn't let me miss any lectures, and always turned the hourglass over for me when I studied at home.

I passed my exams, and Mathew responded to treatment. I got a job in banking and Mathew said he'd decided to go back and complete his final year.

Then it got rather complicated when I forgot what my dad had said, over four years ago, about *being careful*, and I had to tell Mathew about the baby.

Six months after Mathew junior was born, I was alone.

I think my son has an "egg timer" personality. I don't know any other baby who's so fast, or so bright. I think I'll have to persuade him to slow down occasionally and savour the good things in life.

Sometimes, when I look at the sand running through the hourglass, I wonder if there's a way to tip it right over so that time could go backwards. Then I could meet Mathew all over again.

And I'd not waste one minute of our precious time together.

FROM THE AUTHOR

"I've now retired from nursing, and with teenagers flying the nest, I've found plenty of time to indulge my passion for writing."

Teatime Treats

SWEET, CREAMY TREAT

White Chocolate Millionaire's Shortbread

Ingredients

- 450g (1lb) plain flour, sifted
- 2tsp ground ginger
- 125g (4oz) golden caster sugar
- 225g (8oz) salted butter, softened and diced

For The Filling And Topping:

- 450g (1lb) caramel condensed milk
- 250g (9oz) good-quality white chocolate

Preparation time: 30mins + 1hr cooling
Cooking time: 35mins
Makes: 24-30

LOOKS IMPRESSIVE

- Pre-heat oven to 180˚C, Fan Oven 160˚C, Gas Mark 4. Lightly butter a 23x33cm (9x13inch) swiss roll tin.
- Using a food mixer, mix the flour, ginger and sugar together, then add the butter to form a dough. Once it comes together, press it into the prepared tin using the back of a metal spoon to level the top. Prick all over with a fork and bake for 30-35mins or until pale golden. Remove from the oven and cool in the tin.
- To make the filling, gently warm the condensed milk in a small pan, then pour evenly over the shortbread base which will still be slightly warm. Leave to cool and set for about 30mins.
- Melt the white chocolate in a heatproof bowl over a pan of hot water and pour it over the caramel. Leave to set or chill and do not cut before completely cold, about 30mins. Cut into squares with a sharp knife dipped in very hot water and remove from the tin.

RECIPE/STYLING: MAXINE CLARK
PHOTOGRAPHY: LIGHTHOUSE PHOTOGRAPHY

Small Step For

You'll be as amazed as Mary when you find out who's on the other end of the telephone line!

By David Barton

A lmost the second Mary arrived home from shopping and dumped the bags on the work top, her mobile phone rang. She pressed the button to accept the call, but before she could answer, a most peculiar American voice came from the phone. There was a lot of static and the voice came and went.

"Hello? Is there anyone there?" the voice said. "Is there anyone there? This is an emergency!"

"Hello, you're speaking to Mary Brown," Mary said.

"Oh, thank goodness," the voice said. "Where are you speaking to me from?"

"I'm speaking from Derby," she answered as clearly as she could.

"Derby where?"

"Derby in England, of course," she replied.

"England, great! Well, we're the

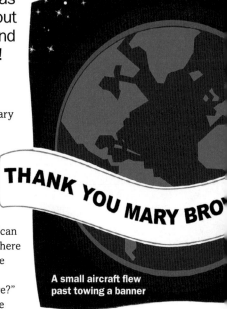

A small aircraft flew past towing a banner

space shuttle *Discovery* and we're in trouble," the voice said.

Pull the other one, Mary thought, but something in the man's voice rang true.

"Listen, we were just getting ready for re-entry when we were hit by some space debris – it hit our antenna and you are the only signal I can tune to. Do you have a landline phone that you can use to

A Woman...

pass on my messages without cutting me off?"

"I have a landline phone with a speaker on it. You may be able to hear each other if I get through."

"Brilliant!" the astronaut said. "Now we don't have much time. *Discovery* will soon be out of range. Take down this number; it'll put you straight

controller, who demanded to know how she knew the code word.

"I have a man on my mobile phone who says he is in a space shuttle and that something has smashed his antenna. I'm the only one he can get on his radio. I'm going to put my mobile and this phone on loudspeaker – I hope you can hear each other!"

Mary did, and soon the two American voices were in frantic conversation with each other. They were talking about telemetery-watsits and altitudes and OMS thrusters and all-sorts. Eventually they did a time check and agreed an OMS time and then they lost contact, as the space craft went out of range.

"Can you hear me now, ma'am?" The mission controller wanted her.

Soon, the two American voices were in frantic conversation with each other

through to NASA." He gave her the number and said she should use the code word "albatross".

Mary dialled the number and once she said the magic word, she was put through to the Kennedy Space Center and a frantic mission

"Yes, I can," she replied, feeling important all of a sudden.

"Well, on behalf of those astronauts up there, and us here at the Kennedy Space Center, I want to thank you. You've set the scene for a spacecraft to safely get home.

That means if the re-entry is fine, as it should be now, you have saved four men's lives and millions of dollars in money."

"Oh, my gosh," Mary said in disbelief. "Please tell me one thing, what is OMS time. I've heard of GMT, Double Summer time and others, but never OMS time."

"OMS, ma'am, is the Orbital

was your day? Mine was terrible!"

"Well, I spoke to the Kennedy Space Center," she said, "and saved a spaceship and its crew."

"That's nice, dear," he said absent-mindedly as he flicked through the post and wandered off to have a shower.

After tea, the boys had some studying to do and Mary and Tom

"Could you give me your details? We'd like to send you a little thank you"

Manoeuvring System, and the time is when the crew must fire the engines to come back to earth in the right place."

"Oh, my word," Mary exclaimed.

"Now, ma'am, could you give me your full name and address? We'd like to send you a little thank you."

Mary gave the man her details, rang off, then set about putting the shopping away.

It wasn't long before her two boys came home from school, crashing through the door, immediately plundering the biscuit tin, asked what time tea was and disappearing again – all this without so much as a kiss, or "Hello, Mum."

Mary finished putting the shopping away and started getting the tea ready. A little while later, Tom, her husband, came home.

"Hello, darling," he said. "How

washed up together. When they had finished, they sat and watched the news. There was an item about the space shuttle having a problem, but that it was resolved and the craft had landed safely.

"A very nice bunch of lads," Mary said.

"Ah, yes, you mentioned it when I came home. Did you hear it on the news?"

Mary thought for a moment.

"Yes, dear," she replied.

The next day was a Saturday and the boys were out the front playing football and Tom was in the back garden, mowing the lawn. He had just come in to make himself a cup of coffee when the two boys came crashing into the house.

"Mum, Mum! There's a

huge car out the front and an American man in uniform asking to see you," they shouted together.

"Well, don't just stand there, ask him in, and put the kettle on again, dear," she said, turning to Tom.

"Wow, cool," seemed to be all the boys could say, and even Tom was dumbstruck.

"Mary Brown?" the man asked.

"Yes," Mary said. "Please come in and sit down."

"It's a great privilege to meet you and your family, ma'am."

"What is this all about?" Tom asked, getting his voice back.

" I see you've been hiding your light under a bushel, ma'am. Well,

"Is there anyone there?"

sir, this good lady of yours picked up an emergency call from our spacecraft and contacted Kennedy. We were then able to get the craft back to earth safely."

"Wow," the boys said in awe.

"Amazing," Tom said. "I thought you were joking yesterday."

"If I may continue, ma'am, we at Kennedy would like to repay you in some small way. We would like, at a time of your choice, to take you and your whole family to the States for a holiday to see the Kennedy Space Center.

"The whole trip would take about three weeks and if you take this phone number and give us a week's notice, we will do everything. A car would pick you up from your door and drop you back here. If you let me know your passport numbers, we will deal with immigration and customs."

"Well, that would be wonderful," Mary said, amazed.

"Wow, cool!" the boys said.

"Well, I am owed some time off from work," Tom said.

"Thank you," Mary said to the American. "You're too generous."

"My pleasure, ma'am!" the American said. "Now, I must go."

W ell, what do you make of that?" Mary said after the American had gone on his way.

"I've got a wife of hidden depths," Tom said with a grin.

Over the next few days, their

"We at Kennedy would like to repay you in some small way"

Over the next few days, their world changed as the media descended

whole world changed. The media descended on their house and Mary even sold her story to a Sunday newspaper – so that was the spending money sorted! They arranged for their holiday to be in a week's time and busied themselves getting ready.

The morning arrived and so did a huge stretch limousine. All their baggage was loaded for them and they were whisked away to a local airfield where an executive jet took them off on their holiday.

Over the three weeks, they were first taken shopping in New York, then spent two days at the Kennedy Space Center where they met the crew of the space shuttle that Mary had saved and had a complete tour of the facility.

They saw the launch of a shuttle mission, then headed to Disney World for the rest of their time. On the way home they stopped in Washington and Mary was thanked by the President for saving the space craft and its crew.

As they went out to the awaiting jet to go home, a small aircraft flew past towing a banner reading *America loves Mary Brown*.

"And so do I," Tom declared as he planted a gentle kiss on his wife's cheek.

ILLUSTRATIONS: ISTOCKPHOTO, INGLIS THORBURN

Fancy That!

Fascinating facts that make you go "wow"!

Little Richard

Peter Sellers, star of the *Pink Panther* films, was actually named Richard Henry Sellers

Fact!
Lady's Smock (Cardamine pratensis) is also known as the cuckoo flower

WOW! ● The pink-footed goose (Anser brachyrhynchus) is the most common grey goose in Britain.

● The roots of your teeth are typically twice as long as the amount of tooth protruding from your gums.

● The common prawn and brown shrimp are a semi-transparent grey-brown and only turn pink when they are cooked.

● According to tooth prints discovered in a piece of birch resin, teenagers have been chewing gum for at least 9000 years.

WOW! ● The crab spider sits in flowers to catch its prey and changes colour from white to yellow or pink to match the petals.

Any Colour...
Rock group *Pink Floyd* took their name from famous blues singers Pink Anderson and Floyd Council

PICTURES: ALAMY, GAP PHOTOS, ISTOCKPHOTO, REX FEATURES, THE MOVIESTORE COLLECTION
WORDS: DOUGLAS MCPHERSON

The House Of Dolls...

Grace was always fascinated with her Aunt Jane's beautiful dolls' house – but what was its secret?

By Mary Williams

The best and worst thing about visiting Aunt Jane and Uncle Charlie was the dolls' house, Grace thought. The best, because it was a beautiful dolls' house with its red brick façade, gabled roof, tall chimneys and bay windows; the worst because she wasn't allowed to play with it. "It's not a toy," Mother would say when Grace complained. But, of course, it *was*

But Grace knew that she did, because the dolls were always in different rooms whenever she visited. Sometimes they would be sitting around the kitchen table, at other times the dark, handsome, moustached father doll and the pretty, brown-haired mother doll would be sitting in the living-room while the small girl with curly, blonde hair and the chubby baby boy sat at their feet. Other times they would all be in their beds. Yes, Grace knew for sure that Aunt Jane

Surprisingly, the dolls were always in different rooms whenever she visited

a toy – what else was it? There was even a family of dolls inside that Grace longed to play with. "But Aunt Jane plays with it," Grace replied petulantly.

Mother laughed. "Of course she doesn't, don't be silly!"

definitely played with the dolls.

Years later Grace took her fiancé, David, to meet Jane and Charlie. While Charlie showed David the garden, Jane and Grace made the tea and chatted.

She so longed to
play with it…

Grace noticed that Jane still had the dolls' house. She asked how long Jane had owned it. "As long as I can remember," Jane replied. "It's an exact replica of the house I used to live in as a girl."

"And the dolls?" Grace asked "Did they come with it?"

Jane looked startled for a second and then replied, "No, they've been there since I was eight – oh, look! There's Charlie and David coming back up, better get that tea poured." Charlie and David came back in then, laughing and joking. All talk of the dolls' house was forgotten. But before Grace left she couldn't resist sneaking a look through the windows. The boy was in his cot, the girl in her bed and the adult dolls were in the living-room.

Grace and David moved away after their marriage and contact with Charlie and Jane was mostly limited to Christmas and birthday cards. Grace's mother kept her up to date with family news and when Uncle Charlie died, Grace and David attended the funeral. After the service they went back to Jane's cottage. The dolls' house still stood on the hall table. Glancing in, Grace noticed the dolls were gathered together at a downstairs window, looking out, as if expecting a visitor to arrive.

Poor Jane had lost all her family in a house fire when she was just eight

A new doll had appeared…

Jane seemed lost and confused without Charlie. On impulse Grace said, "You would be very welcome to come and stay with us, Aunt Jane."

"Perhaps I will." Jane smiled.

It was the last time Grace saw Jane alive. On the day of the funeral Grace learned that she was a beneficiary in Jane's will. Jane had left her the dolls' house.

M other greeted Grace at the door of Jane's cottage. "Come in, have a cup of tea. I was just sorting through some old photos." While Mother made tea, Grace hung her coat up. Looking through the dolls' house windows she saw that the dolls were in the living room. Grace was surprised to see that another doll had been added to the collection, a pretty girl doll with long, dark plaits. Where had Aunt Jane got it from?

"Tea's ready," said Mother. "Admiring your dolls' house?" she asked, moving to the hall.

"Yes," replied Grace, "Aunt Jane must have put another doll in; there are five of them now." Mother looked puzzled " I don't think there are any dolls in there."

"Yes, there have always been dolls in there," said Grace.

"No, you must be seeing things, I was looking at it earlier, there are no dolls – look!" She removed the

front of the house. It was empty! Grace stared in disbelief. They had all gone! It wasn't possible. "They were there," said Grace. "Just now."

Her mother looked doubtful. "I think we'd better have that cup of tea." Grace followed her mother into the kitchen.

Untidy piles of black and white photographs lay on the table. Grace picked one up – it was a family portrait.

"I was just looking at that," said Mother. "Unfortunately, it was the only photograph that Jane had of her family; it must have been taken not long before the fire."

"Fire?" Grace queried.

"Yes, didn't I tell you? Poor Jane lost all her family in a house fire when she was just eight years old."

Grace felt suddenly cold; a closer look at the picture showed a dark, handsome, moustached man, his pretty wife holding a chubby male toddler, a little girl with bouncy blonde curls and an older girl with dark eyes and long, dark plaits – it was Jane.

FROM THE AUTHOR

"Many years ago I visited a toy museum in South Wales. A legend attached to a dolls' house gave me the inspiration for this story."

ILLUSTRATIONS: ALAMY, MANDY DIXON

Memories Of Venice

Thoughts of lovers lost will come back to you, too, as you enjoy this touching tale of self discovery

By Barbara Dynes

Bernie's a great teacher, isn't he?" Grace Hoskins enthused. "Arranging outings like this to exhibitions. Pete never did!"

"True," Janice answered, gazing around the massive hall, its walls displaying countless paintings. To be honest, after wandering around for over an hour, she was getting more depressed by the minute. The more she saw of others' work,

back and content to let her just enjoy her painting. This new one was much more critical.

"I reckon it's time we did some work," Grace said, making a beeline for a bench. Janice groaned as she followed her friend.

"Bring your sketchbooks and have a go at copying some of the artists' styles," they'd been instructed. "It does no harm to copy. You can learn a lot."

Well, she might learn a lot, but her pictures never seemed to

The most poignant episodes of her life had taken place in this unique city

the more she realised just how bad she was, despite the fact that she'd been enjoying art for more years than she cared to remember. There was something to be said for Pete, their first art teacher, who'd now retired. He was much more laid

improve, much as she loved doing them. Not that it really mattered, she told herself. She painted purely for pleasure. After her dear Tom had died two years ago, going back to art classes had given her a new lease of life. If only, just once, she

Where had the romance gone?

could turn out something promising. Perhaps today would be the day!

Janice gazed at the painting facing her. It was a picture of gondolas on a canal in Venice – all muted colours, as though seen through a mist. Her mood changed and she suddenly felt quite weepy. Not just because of the beauty of the painting – though that was reason enough. But… Venice! One of the most poignant episodes of her life had taken place in that unique city. A turning point, you might call it. She fidgeted on the hard bench.

"You okay?" Grace asked, looking up from her drawing. "You look a bit harassed!"

"No, I'm fine," Janice answered. "I think I'll do the Venetian scene."

"I shall go for the abstract," Grace declared. "All those dots fascinate me!"

Janice looked at the picture to the left of the gondolas. It was made up of hundreds of multi-coloured dots and a few squiggles. Ironic, she thought. Venice and modern art sitting side by side… Attempting to draw the shape of a gondola, she sighed. Maybe this wasn't a good picture to have chosen. It just brought back painful memories of the Venice of forty years ago…

How excited she'd been, signing up for that painting holiday! Only ever having been as far as France, she was thrilled with the idea of seeing Italy – and especially Venice. But the real bonus had been the presence of Alex, one of the other art students. Tall, dark Alex – a happy-go-lucky type – was an apprentice engineer. Janice had only been out with him a few times, but she was completely besotted. Just being in the same room with him had made her feel quite light-headed! Never before had anyone had such an effect on her.

Now, Janice bent her head closer to her drawing, in case the emotion showed in her face. Crazy, she told herself, a woman in her sixties reliving her emotional past! But all those years ago, something had clicked between her and Alex. Both young and enthusiastic, they'd got on so well in spite of having opposite tastes in everything. He liked horror films, she adored musicals; he was a football fanatic, she hated it; he worshipped the Rolling Stones while she was a Beatles fan. Then there was the art…

Grace broke into her thoughts.

"I'm going dotty here!" she said, chewing the end of her pencil. "I think I might have chosen the wrong picture to copy."

Janice smiled.

"You're not the only one! How

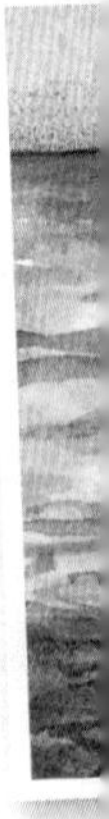

Alex, she couldn't be doing with his favourite style of art: abstract, they called it.

"I don't slosh paint about," Alex protested. "Everyone should try modern art! Ask Beryl about it…"

"No, thanks!" Janice had cried, jerking bolt upright. How could he dare to bring Beryl Jones into the argument! Beryl might be a first class artist – oils, watercolour, traditional, modern – you name it,

How did you draw a gondola?

Even after 40 years, memories of Venice were still so vivid and bittersweet

d'you draw a gondola? Mine looks like a tipped-up banana!"

Grace peered at Janice's effort.

"Try shading it in. That'll help!"

Janice stared at the picture on the wall. It was beautiful; the mist, the water, the hazy sunshine… was there ever a more romantic setting? she wondered dreamily. Two people relaxing in a gondola, with a swarthy Italian serenading them! She closed her eyes and was back in the heady heat of Venice.

"Beautiful, isn't it?" she'd said to Alex that day as she lay back in the gondola, gazing at the azure sky. "I wish I could do all this justice with my painting…"

"You should try going modern," Alex suggested.

"What? Slosh paint about, like you do? No way!" Janice retorted indignantly. Much as she adored

she was an expert, but that was not the point. "I think rubbish like that in this magical setting is nothing short of criminal!" she declared.

And that was just the start. The argument had got stronger and stronger – their voices echoing over the water, shattering the peaceful atmosphere. People stared in astonishment as the classic romantic setting turned really ugly. That poor gondolier must have been tempted to tip them both into the water!

Janice frowned now. After all these years, she could still picture that scene – a fuming Alex defending his art, all the while dabbing away at beads of sweat running down the sides of his face with a hanky. She shuddered. How could she have been so arrogant!

After all, Alex had never once criticised her terrible stuff. "You're too outspoken for words!" her mother had warned. "You'll get your comeuppance one day!"

Mum was right. From then on, Alex had cooled towards her, opting to sit with the blonde, pretty Beryl. He'd stayed friendly enough, but Janice knew that she'd lost out.

Later, back home, she had wanted so much to make it up with him. But, even in those swinging, hippy days, girls still hesitated to take the initiative. Before she could find the courage to act, he qualified as an engineer and moved away from the area.

"Ah, interesting!" A voice from behind brought her back to the present. "A wonderful place, Venice!" Bernie observed.

"True," Janice murmured, flushing bright red. She felt really guilty – sitting here concentrating on her memories.

"The picture needs more life," Bernie went on, studying Janice's drawing. "Try concentrating on the couple in the gondola."

Then, turning to Grace's effort, "Ah, now, I like that! A bit more to the left with that line, though. Bring the sketches in to class next week, ladies!" he added, moving on.

Exasperated, Janice stared at her pitiful effort. "More life," he'd said. Right! She got out her rubber and began rubbing away furiously.

"Steady on, woman!" Grace giggled. "You'll have no paper left!"

Janice was past caring. She quickly sketched in two very large figures, then took a deep breath.

"I'm thinking of quitting this class, Grace," she declared. "I might take up pottery. Wrestling with clay is more my thing!"

"But you can't… You love art –"

"But I can't do it!" Janice sighed.

Ten minutes later, she sat back, blinking at her hastily scrawled picture. Grace also stopped drawing to look.

"Janice, that's heaps better –"

"You would say that, now!" Janice laughed.

"But it is! I challenge you to bring that along next week," Grace said. "See what Bernie says about it."

It needed more life…

"I know exactly what he'll say." Janice pulled a face, then shrugged. "Oh, okay, why not?"

Janice felt at odds with the entire world. Remembering Venice had thrown her somewhat. Which was crazy, because she'd had a wonderful marriage with Tom – she didn't regret a moment of it.

some kind of masochist, putting herself through all this!

"A good portrait – well done, George!" Bernie said, going on to comment on several others. "Ah, what have we here?" Janice grimaced as she recognised the worn, crumpled paper he held up.

"Two people having a row in a

"Your sketch has really come alive. You feel for that couple in the gondola"

Their caring, married daughter, Imogen, might live miles away, but she was always on the phone, especially since Tom died.

"Why not come and live up here, Mum?" she'd suggested. But Janice didn't want to move. She had her friends, her swimming and her art. "Wouldn't it be great if you met someone else?" Imogen said once. "Dad wouldn't have wanted you to be lonely."

Janice sighed. It all seemed so unfair to Tom's memory…

A t the following art class, all the students' sketches from their exhibition work was laid out on a long table. Janice had almost chickened out, but Grace insisted.

After a general discussion about the exhibition, Bernie grinned.

"Right! It's time to look at these masterpieces!"

Janice watched nervously as he scrutinised their work. She must be

gondola! Great expressions, especially his! They both look furious!" He laughed. "I like the embarrassed gondolier in the background… and the grey shading of the canal water. This is really good, Janice!" he added.

Janice gulped. He was actually praising her!

"You've made it come alive," the tutor went on. "I'd say you really felt for that couple!"

She nodded. More than you will ever know, she thought wryly.

Grace piped up. "Janice is threatening to leave the class. Perhaps you could have a word with her. Bernie?"

"Okay! Do stay afterwards, Janice," he said, as he moved on to the next drawing.

L ater, sitting alone with Bernie – alias Alex Bernard – Janice felt like a nervous teenager. She had tried to avoid any personal contact with him since he'd first walked into the classroom and she had sat there, speechless with surprise. After all, forty years had gone by! They were different people now.

"When I moved back to this area and took over the class, I couldn't believe my luck, seeing you again, Janice," he said hesitantly. "I

Atmosphere and romance

She now knew the awe she'd felt for him all those years ago had never left

always regretted letting you go. My own silly pride was to blame!"

Janice blushed, looking away.

"I owe you an apology," he went on. "That day Grace joked about me being a bachelor and saying you were both 'merry widows', I jumped the gun by asking you out to dinner. I'm so sorry…"

"It didn't seem right at the time," Janice said. "But now –"

She stopped. Gazing into his brown eyes, she realised that some of the awe she'd felt for him years ago was still there. It had been since that first day…

"Are you really leaving the class, Janice?" Alex asked anxiously.

"No! Not now there's a glimmer of hope for me as an artist!"

She laughed. Of course, there was another reason why quitting had never really been an option:

having Alex as her teacher…

"And I would like to have dinner with you, please," she added. "I have to find some way of making up for my behaviour that day on the gondola!"

"I was just as bad. Put it down to youth and high-spirits!"

Janice smiled up at him. She actually quite liked modern art these days. But, in her view, a romantic painted picture of Venice would always triumph over one made up of dots.

ABOUT THE AUTHOR

"My ideas come from family life and holidays. Working out the plot can be difficult. That can take longer than actually writing the story!"

Teatime Treats

QUICK, EASY MAKE

Jammy Flapjacks

FILLING TREAT

Ingredients
- 200g (7oz) salted butter, plus extra for buttering
- 6tbsp golden syrup
- 450g (1lb) porridge oats
- 1 large egg, beaten
- ½ jar jam

Preparation time: 20mins
Cooking time: 25mins
Makes: approx 24

● Pre-heat oven to 180˚C, Fan Oven 160˚C, Gas Mark 4. Evenly butter the base and sides of an 18x27cm (7x11inch) swiss roll tin.

● Melt the **butter** and **syrup** together in a large pan over a low heat. Stir in half the **oats**, the beaten **egg**, then the remaining oats and mix well to thoroughly coat in the butter and egg mixture.

● Tip half into the prepared tin and spread out evenly. Carefully spread this with the jam. Dot spoonfuls of the remaining oat mixture over the jam, spreading out to cover it completely. Bake for 20-25mins or until light golden-brown but still slightly soft.

● Cut into bars or squares while still hot, then allow to cool completely on a wire rack before removing from the tin. Store in an airtight tin.

RECIPE/STYLING: MAXINE CLARK
PHOTOGRAPHY: LIGHTHOUSE PHOTOGRAPHY

The Jubilee

By Robert Aldridge

Both PC Harry Pegg and WPC "Jenny" Wren pushed their way through the small flea-market crowd to where a man in his seventies stood, his back to the wall, holding aloft a defiant walking stick. His other hand gripped a pack of cigarette cards.

Sitting on the floor nearby was a younger man with a bloodstained handkerchief pressed to his nose; between them the wreck of a trestle table and a scattering of old comics, picture postcards and gramophone records littered the floor. Harry decided to dispense with the "'Ello-ello" and opened with the "What's-all-this-then?"

The seated man moved the handkerchief aside and pointed accusingly at the other.

"Arrest him, Constable. Look what he's done to my nose – and he nicked them fag cards."

"No, I never," the older man growled. "You tipped the table up yourself trying to grab 'em off me. It hit him right on the conk." The older man looked at Harry with a grimace of satisfaction.

Harry then decided to ask the injured man his name.

"Stibbins – Reginald Stibbins."

Jenny wrote it down and looked at the man with the stick.

"Francis William Johnson," he said. "And I never nicked these cards." He pointed his stick at Stibbins, who flinched. "He's the dirty, rotten thief here!"

Harry held out his hand.

"May I see? Thank you." He riffled through the cards. "Racing drivers, eh? I take it these were sitting on the stall? How do you think they got there?"

"I just said, didn't I?" Johnson pointed his stick at Stibbins again.

"Arrest him, Constable. Look what he's done – and he nicked them fag cards"

"He pinched 'em – honest, he did."

"Where did he take them from, Mr Johnson?" Jenny asked.

Johnson took his time answering and eventually it was quietly and with great bitterness.

"Twenty-three Trafalgar Street."

Tin

Coming across a crime scene with one victim claiming theft, the other assault, who would *you* believe?

Collectors' items?

"He's barmy," Stibbins said, still dabbing with the handkerchief. "Is it still bleeding?" he asked.

"You'll live, Mr Stibbins," Harry said. "Can you tell me when this was, Mr Johnson?"

Johnson fell quiet, until Jenny prompted him. "Mr Johnson?"

"I'm not sure… not exactly."

"Well, now," Harry said. "We've got two allegations of theft and one of assault. I think we'll have to sort it out down at the station."

A little later, PCs Pegg and Wren shared an interview room with Frank Johnson. The small pack of cigarette cards lay on the table.

"We'll just keep it informal for now, Mr Johnson," Harry said. "Mr Stibbins said you took these cards from his stall. Is that true?"

Johnson nodded and scowled.

"I was entitled to. I collected them cards meself. It took me ages to get a set together."

Jenny picked up a card showing a pre-war English Racing Automobile in British racing green.

"I suppose this was a long time ago, Mr Johnson."

"In the Thirties," Johnson replied. "When I was a lad."

"And you say they were taken from…" Harry looked down at his notes. "Twenty-three Trafalgar Street… but you're not sure when. Is that your present address?"

"'Course not." Johnson looked at him with scorn. "There hasn't been a Trafalgar Street since before the Blitz. It's all different round here now."

Harry leaned back in his chair.

"Mr Stibbins couldn't have taken them then, could he?" he said. "I doubt if he would even have been born in those days."

"P'raps I was a bit hasty there." Johnson looked embarrassed. "You could do him for receiving stolen goods, though, officer?"

I reckon that is debatable," Harry said. "It depends how he came by them. Was the, er, theft reported at the time?"

There was a long silence from Johnson before he finally elaborated.

"I was in Burma when the house went – mother, father, our Josie and Eileen, little Billy… and our gran – all dead."

There was silence again and Jenny had to blink hard.

"Then I was wounded and taken prisoner," Johnson went on. "It was 1946 before I got home, and d'you know what I found? Weeds, that's all. No Trafalgar Street, no Balaclava Street, no Waterloo Street." There was bitterness in his voice. "They'd even cleared all the rubble away. Just weeds."

"And these went missing when the bomb hit your house." Harry tapped the little pack of cards. "Is that what you are saying?"

"Yes, must have."

"So you are no longer accusing

"It was 1946 before I made it home, and even the rubble had been cleared away!"

Was there anything left?

Mr Stibbins of the theft of these?"

Johnson shook his head wearily.

"Can I have another look?"

Jenny pushed the cards across and Johnson spread them, face up, with a gentle stroke of his hand.

"You can't imagine what it was like," he said. "Seeing these on that stall. It made me wobble a bit, know what I mean? I thought… If I walk outside everything will be like it was. All the old 'ouses will still be there and our gran'll come walking down the street with her shoppin' – Billy holding 'er hand…" He stopped speaking, eyes shut tight.

With her little finger, Jenny carefully removed a spot of moisture from her cheek. Harry cleared his throat.

"There must have been loads of these printed, Mr Johnson; what makes you think these are yours?"

Johnson tapped a card with a gnarled forefinger. "John Cobb driving a Railton. Turn it over and tell me what's on the rear."

Jenny turned the card over. "A lot of printing and a big ink blot."

"And who does the ink blot remind you of?"

Jenny wrinkled her brow. Harry twisted his head for a better look.

"I know," Harry said. "Queen Victoria!" He noticed Jenny's look of doubt.

"Exactly," Johnson said. "I know they're mine because I remember that blot." He swept the cards up like a poker player and sat back. "Do I keep 'em?"

"Ah, well, strictly speaking, they're still evidence," Harry said, "We've got to have a word with Mr Stibbins now."

Johnson handed over the pack with reluctance.

A little later, Stibbins took Frank Johnson's place in the interview room. Jenny asked him how his nose was. He touched it with care.

"Sore," he said. "Have you charged him, then?"

"Mr Johnson? Well, no," Harry said. "He says that you leaned on the trestle and it hit you."

"Yeah, well, that was down to him, wasn't it? I mean, if he hadn't tried to nick half me stock…"

"The cigarette cards," Jenny jumped in to correct him.

"Yeah, well, the cigarette cards, I

suppose I should be saying."

"Did he actually try to walk off with them?" Harry asked, "Maybe he just wanted to take a closer look at them – prior to making you an offer for them."

Stibbins snorted, then winced and dabbed his nose once more.

"Make me an offer? No way!" he said. "He never actually walked off, but 'e was yelling they was his and calling me names an' that."

Harry tilted his chair back and drummed his fingers on the table in front of him.

"So!" he said. "No theft attempt and no blows struck. This looks like it could be a bit of a waste of police time, I reckon."

The sullen Stibbins now looked very uncomfortable.

"Look," he said. "He's probably a bit, you know, dotty. What say we forget the whole thing, eh? I'm losing money stuck here."

Jenny sighed, tapping the cards.

"But there's still the question of who owns these," she said and turned over the John Cobb. "You see, Mr Johnson recognised this ink blot. He says it looks just like his paternal grandmother."

"What a shame for her." Stibbins was unable to hold back a snigger.

"Yes," Harry said. "It is a shame. Poor gran. She was killed when a bomb hit Mr Johnson's house – along with the rest of his family."

"Mr Johnson was in Burma when it happened," Jenny added,

"then he was wounded and taken prisoner… It's a really sad story, when you start to think about it."

"Lots o' blokes was wounded at the time." Stibbins sneered again unsympathetically. "There was a war on, don't you know…"

"No… I mean the cards. D'you know, they're the only thing he's ever found from his old home? The only thing that can connect him to his family?"

"You're wringing my heart strings." Stibbins's lip curled. "All right, all right, he can have the flaming cards."

"That's very warm-hearted of you, Mr Stibbins." Jenny smiled.

"For five quid," Stibbins added.

"Perhaps just lukewarm then," Harry said.

"That ink blot lowers their value in any case." Stibbins got up on to his feet to go.

"Depends where you're standing

They had all gone…

doesn't it?" Harry rose as well, patting his pockets. "Er, have you got any money on you, Jen?"

An hour later, PCs Pegg and Wren were back pounding the pavement. "What say we take a peek in the flea market again?" Harry suggested. "Make sure it's

had a thick rubber band round it made from an old inner tube."

Stibbins was furious; he pulled the biscuit tin closer.

"I tell you, I bought this lot at auction – and there weren't no rubber band round it!"

"There was, but it perished away." They all immediately turned to

"I tell you, I bought this lot at auction – and there weren't no rubber band!"

all quiet after all the excitement."

"That's probably a good idea."

When they stepped into the market hall it was apparent that all was definitely not quiet. Stibbins and Frank Johnson were bickering and arguing again.

"Is everything all right with you, Mr Johnson?" Jenny asked.

"No, it damned well isn't." He was red-faced and angry. Johnson pointed to a large careworn biscuit tin that was decorated brightly with painted flags and bore the portraits of King George V and Queen Mary with the dates *1910-1935* very prominently displayed.

"I never noticed before, what with all the kerfuffle. The swine's got me whole bloomin' collection – look! Butterflies, cricketers, film stars – the lot! I kept 'em all in that Jubilee tin. It

the bright-eyed elderly lady who had volunteered this small titbit of hitherto unknown information.

"And you are, madam?" Jenny opened her notebook.

"Joan McGuire – Mrs – and it was me who put those cards in the auction. Jubilee tin and all."

Stibbins said, "Told you so." Harry then asked her how she'd come by the cards in the first place. Mrs McGuire said that the tin had come flying through her window at five past two on the morning of February 2, 1943, and had nearly killed her. She bent her head and parted her hair with her fingers.

"I've still got the scar, look." She fixed Johnson with a glare. "And if you're Frankie Johnson, you ought to be ashamed."

"What for? I didn't throw it!"

"There was a note in that box… from Millie Hodges."

Johnson's jaw dropped. "Goodness gracious! Not her from

Where real history is made…

Hill Street seniors…!"

Mrs McGuire nodded knowingly now.

"I hope your mother never read it."

Johnson frantically grabbed the box back and started to scrabble through the contents.

"It's not still in here, is it?" he asked, anxious now as to where the evidence could be.

"Don't you worry, I gave it back to Millie years ago."

"I don't remember a Joan McGuire." Johnson glared at her.

"I was Joanie Price in those days."

"Joanie Price?" A sunshine smile spread all across Johnson's face.

of the thinning crowds. Harry put on his profound look and gestured with his thumb back towards the flea market.

"'That's what real history is about, Jen. Never mind your dates

"Joanie Price? From the little sweet shop in Jamaica Street? Well, I'll be…"

"From the little sweet shop in Jamaica Street ? Well, I'll be…"

Stibbins's scowl lightened a few degrees. In fact, he almost smiled.

"My mum was born in Jamaica Street," he said.

Frank Johnson and Joan McGuire were grinning at each other now. Harry caught Jenny's eye and they edged away from the stall.

"I reckon we can leave them to sort it, now," Harry said.

Outside in the street, awnings were coming down and brooms were being plied round the ankles

and your kings and queens. Real history is all about ordinary people; the little dramas and crises that impact on their everyday lives and loves."

"And notes from Millie Hodges…" Jenny chuckled. "I'd love to know what it said…"

FROM THE AUTHOR

"Stir up old enthusiasms and you never know what will float to the surface."

ILLUSTRATIONS: JAMES DEWAR

Teatime Treats

Sticky Toffee Chocolate Brownies

FUN CHOCCY TREAT

Ingredients

- 250g (9oz) pitted soft dried dates, finely chopped
- 50g (2oz) cocoa powder
- 125g (4oz) butter
- 250g (9oz) dark brown sugar
- 2 eggs, beaten
- 175g (6oz) self-raising flour
- 18 Rolos

Preparation time: 20mins + cooling
Cooking time: 25-30mins
Makes: 18 squares

- Pre-heat oven to 180°C, Fan Oven 160°C, Gas Mark 4. Grease and line an 18x28cm (7x11inch) oblong cake tin.
- Put the dates in a large pan with 250ml (9fl oz) water, the cocoa, butter and sugar. Heat very gently, stirring, until completely melted together. Cool for 10mins. Stir in the egg and sift over the flour. Carefully mix together, then pour into the prepared tin. Push the Rolos into surface of the mixture at regular intervals.
- Bake for 25-35mins until risen and just firm to the touch. Allow to cool in the tin before cutting into 18 squares.

SWEET AND TASTY

RECIPE/STYLING: KATHRYN HAWKINS
PHOTOGRAPHY: UPFRONT PHOTOGRAPHY

Helping Hands

Christmas is a time for friends and families and for passing traditions from one generation to the next…

By Ginny Swart

annah loved babysitting four-year-old Ethan. She didn't mean to spoil her grandson, but she couldn't help buying him little gifts. She had already collected a lot of stocking fillers for Christmas: little metal motorcars, puzzles, plastic farm animals and a beautiful spinning top that hummed and whistled. *I must tell Trish that I've bought all that*, she thought, *no point in duplicating.*

Her daughter, Trish, was coming round that evening to drop off her grandson while she and Jeff went to see a film, and Hannah planned to put up and decorate her small tree with him to help her.

She decided it would also be a good opportunity to unpack the little wooden nativity set that she'd had since Trish was a little girl.

But when Trish came round later with Jeff, she said, "Mum, you remember those old wooden figures for the Christmas crib? D'you think I could have them this year? I want to make a little crib scene at home for Ethan. He's just the right age to help set it up."

"Oh…" One look at Trish's happy expectant face made Hannah say, "Of course, darling. I've got it all packed away in a box, I'll get it for you."

She gently brought it down from the cupboard and remembered the little stocking fillers in there, too.

She'd made the Christmas pudding every year since she married Harry 30 years ago

grandson while she and Jeff went to see a film, and Hannah planned to put up and decorate her small tree with him to help her.

She decided it would also be a good opportunity to unpack the little wooden nativity set that she'd

"Father Christmas is coming to your house on Christmas Eve as usual, isn't he?" she began. "Because I've –"

"I'll say!" Jeff grinned. "That's if he can stagger up the path with all the stuff Trish has bought."

She wanted everything to be just perfect!

"Oh, go on, Jeff, who was it that bought that set of racing cars? And the whistling top?"

Hannah's heart sank. How could she not have realised they'd also splash out with gifts?

"Oh, dear," she murmured, "I've bought a few things from Father Christmas, too, I'm afraid."

"Well, would you like us to wrap them and pop them in his stocking for when he wakes up on Christmas morning?"

She fetched a few but kept three little cars to wrap and give herself, and left the handsome spinning top where it was.

"And Mum, do you think I could borrow your special red Christmas tablecloth? Jeff's folks are coming and I want things perfect!"

"Of course, sweetheart."

This year Trish had taken over the Christmas dinner planning and arrangements and would probably want to carry on doing it every year. *Which is how it should be,*

I've already made a really big –"

She was about to say "Christmas pudding" but Trish interrupted.

"I've made the most enormous Christmas pudding, Mum," she said. "I used that recipe you gave me because I know it's always a success when you use it. Your puddings are legendary!"

But you never told me you were making the pudding this year as well!

Hannah was silent. She'd made the Christmas pudding every year since – well, since she'd married Harry 30 years before.

When Trish and Jeff had married the year after her husband died, they'd set up home in a tiny flat with no room to entertain. They'd continued coming to her for Christmas dinner and she'd kept all the family traditions going for them. But last year they'd bought a house and almost the first thing Trish had said

"This tree's very pretty, Nana – much better than ours at home," Ethan said

thought Hannah rather wistfully. *Trish is such a good little organiser, but of course I'll always be able to contribute.*

"I'm glad your parents are coming, Jeff, I haven't seen Charles and Margaret for ages," said Hannah cheerfully. "Luckily

when they moved in was "We'll have Christmas dinner at our place this year!" It never occurred to her that this year Trish might want to make her own pudding.

She cleared her throat. "How about mince pies?" she asked, trying to keep the plaintive note

**Every decoration was
a memory for her**

out of her voice. "Shall I make some of them and bring them along?"

"Those are my mum's speciality," said Jeff. "She'll be bringing those."

"So should I make the cake?" Hannah hadn't planned to make one, but she had to bring something!

"Mum, I meant to tell you! I was so lucky – I won a fruitcake in the office raffle! It's beautifully iced and better than anything I could have baked. So you won't have to worry about that."

"Well, I'll bring along the nuts and raisins," said Hannah firmly. "And some chocolate."

"We can never have too many chocolates." Jeff, who had a sweet tooth, grinned. "Come on Trish, we'd better be going if we want to see this film."

"Chocolates?" Ethan wandered through from where he'd been playing with his toys.

"For Christmas. Not now," said Trish firmly. "'Bye, Mum. Be a good boy with Nana, Ethan."

"He's always good," Hannah smiled. "We're going to decorate the tree I bought this afternoon and then have a story before bed, aren't we, Ethan?"

They were happily busy for the next hour, carefully unwrapping the glass balls and sparkly bits, deciding where each piece would go. Ethan worked with his tongue sticking out in concentration, and Hannah wished she'd thought to have a camera handy.

"Oh, I made this one, didn't I, Nana?" He pounced on a cardboard star that he'd decorated the year before, with sequins haphazardly glued onto both sides. "I didn't know you kept it!"

"Of course I did, sweetheart, I love all the things you make." Hannah smiled. "And do you remember making this one?"

She held up an odd shaped lump of something hard, painted bright red with a wire hook protruding. The gold glitter had almost all fallen off. "You made this when you were only two!"

"That's babyish. You should throw it away."

"Never," said Hannah firmly. "Look how pretty it is against the green needles."

Ethan stepped back and looked critically at their handiwork.

"It's very pretty, Nana," he said. "Better than ours. We've got a white one with silver stuff on it. No nice colours."

"I'm sure it's very pretty, too."

Hannah had her own opinion of white plastic Christmas trees, but so far she kept them to herself.

"Now, Master Ethan, I think it's your bedtime."

She tucked him in and read him one of his favourite Brer Rabbit stories and she reflected sadly that she'd hardly ever had time to sit and watch Trish fall asleep like this. *One of the advantages of being a grandmother, I suppose,* she thought. *More time to do the important things!*

At around eight o'clock on Christmas Eve, Jeff popped in rather unexpectedly .

"Crisis!" he said. "We've just had a very hairy moment. Ethan got hold of some matches and thought he'd light a candle under our plastic Christmas tree and the whole thing started to melt."

"Oh, my heavens! Is he hurt?"

"No, luckily I was there and just whipped the thing out of the door before it had a chance to catch fire. But now we're minus one Christmas tree and we were wondering if you could – sort of lend us yours for Christmas Day? My folks are coming and Trish –"

"Wants everything to be perfect!" finished Hannah. "Of course, Jeff. It's quite a small one so I expect it will fit into your car pretty well."

Hannah watched her cheerful little tree being driven away on the back seat and smiled. At least she was helping with the festivities,

even if it wasn't any of the food!

On Christmas morning she arrived at Trish and Jeff's carrying a shopper with her contributions and Christmas gifts. Ethan ran out to greet her.

"Look what Father Christmas brought me, Nana!" He pumped the top vigorously and it spun around with a deep, musical hum.

"Why, what a lucky boy you are. Isn't that lovely?"

"And Mummy and me made a Christmas crib for Baby Jesus! Come and see."

Trish had laid out the little wooden figures on a low cupboard in the hall, and hung a big golden star above. Someone had knitted a clumsy square in red wool, which served as a blanket for the baby.

"Guess who made this blanket, Mum?" Trish said, laughing, as she came up behind her mother and put her arm around her waist. "Ethan! I told him you taught me to

The Christmas table was laden with dishes

knit a square for the crib when I was little and he wanted to do one as well."

"The tree looks very nice." Hannah smiled. "You've found just the right spot for it."

"Much better than that plastic one, too. Thanks so much for coming to our rescue, Mum.

"Now come and say a Christmas like the table Hannah used to set in the days when Trish and her brother had sat down to family Christmas dinners so long ago.

The hour before the meal passed quickly as everyone opened gifts and exclaimed with pleasure over the contents.

Ethan got wildly excited opening them all. Charles and Margaret

"Mum! Disaster!" Trish was distraught. "The Christmas pudding is ruined!"

hello to Charles and Margaret."

Jeff's parents lived in the country and didn't come to town very often. As a result, Trish was still a bit in awe of her mother-in-law who, she was convinced, was ready to sweep her critical eye over all her shortcomings as an inexperienced housekeeper.

"I was just saying to Charles how prettily Trish has done everything for Christmas!" Margaret said. "Such a sweet Christmas tree and a beautiful little crib! And the table set so nicely. She's very creative, isn't she?"

Trish blushed with pleasure and grinned across at her mother. "I had a bit of help from the expert," she said.

Hannah's red cloth was set with their best cutlery and glasses, with fat white candles in the centre wreathed in fresh green ivy. The whole effect was charming, exactly generously gave him an enormous construction set, which Trish put to one side soon after he'd torn off the wrapping paper.

"Three hundred pieces, how wonderful!" she murmured diplomatically. "I think we should put this away until Ethan and Jeff have lots of time to play with it."

Hannah was pleased she'd wrapped the little cars. He played with them immediately, making growling motor-car noises in and out of the grown-ups' legs.

Then interesting smells started to come from the kitchen and Trish got up unobtrusively and slipped off to check on the meal.

"Let me help you, dear." Hannah started to get to her feet but Trish shook her head.

"No, Mum, you stay and chat. Everything's under control."

Honestly, thought Hannah crossly, *I'm not allowed to*

contribute and not allowed to help!

But during a particularly loud burst of laughter at one of Charles's stories, she heard an ominous crash beyond the closed door, and went to investigate.

"Mum! Disaster!" Trish was on her knees, distraught. "I dropped the bowl with the Christmas pudding and it's broken. The pudding's full of glass bits and completely ruined!"

Hannah surveyed the damage. Trish was right, the blobs of pudding were glinting with tiny splinters and nothing could be saved.

"And what on earth can I tell Jeff's Mum? I wanted everything to be perfect!"

Hannah tried not to smile. "No problem," she said. "I just happen to have another one. I'll pop home and fetch it."

"Honestly? How come you made a Christmas pudding when I – oh, no! You'd made it already!"

"Wasn't that lucky? It'll just take me ten minutes."

Jeff ran her home in his car, and they were back with the second pudding before anyone had had time to miss them.

Trish greeted them in relief.

"Do you think you could give me a hand after all, Mum? I've still got to make the gravy."

Together they bustled about Trish's tiny kitchen, dishing vegetables into serving bowls and warming plates.

Just before they went in to the dining room laden with dishes, Trish put down the platter with the turkey on it and gave her mother a huge hug.

"I don't know what I'd do without you, Mum," she whispered. "Everything you've given us and everything you've done… if it wasn't for you, this Christmas dinner would have been a disaster!"

"Don't be daft, love," said Hannah. "I'm just happy to have been able to help. Now let's get Jeff to carve this big fellow and then open some champagne."

"Champagne? Oh no!" Trish clapped her hand to her forehead. "I meant to get some but in all the rushing about –"

"Well, isn't that lucky," Hannah said. "I put a bottle in your fridge when I arrived. I had to contribute something, after all!"

ABOUT THE AUTHOR

"Christmas is about tradition and I wish you a traditional greeting of health, wealth and happiness for Christmas and the New Year."

Relax with **My Weekly**

Favourite **Celebrities** and inspirational women you'll love to read about

Travel to places you want to see in the UK and abroad

Health stories important to you

Delicious **recipes** you can't wait to make

My Weekly

On Sale Every Tuesday

Plus Big-name novelists, super short stories, mini-serials, puzzles, unusual facts and helpful tips